Disney • PIXAR

TURNING RED

The Real
R.P.G.

The Story of the Red Panda Girl

Design by Winnie Ho
Composition and layout by Susan Gerber

Published by Disney Press, an imprint of Buena Vista Books, Inc. No part of this book may be reproduced or transmitted in any form or by any means, electronic or mechanical, including photocopying, recording, or by any information storage and retrieval system, without written permission from the publisher. For information address Disney Press, 1200 Grand Central Avenue, Glendale, California 91201.

Printed in the United States of America
First Hardcover Edition, February 2022
10 9 8 7 6 5 4 3 2 1
FAC-038091-21358

Library of Congress Control Number: 2021944345
ISBN 978-1-368-07579-4

Visit disneybooks.com

DISNEY · PIXAR

TURNING RED

The Real

R.P.G.

The Story of the Red Panda Girl

By Lily Quan

DISNEP PRESS

Los Angeles · New York

"Step, step, turn, and freeze!"

The 4*Townies struck a pose as the music ended. Miriam wailed, "Can we take a break? We've been rehearsing for five hours straight!"

"No way!" said Mei, the leader of the 4*Townies. "We're competing against groups from all over the world. We can't stop if we want to win."

The 4*Townies were the best girl band in the country. Their hit song "Nothing Can Stop Us!" was the number one single in Canada for ten weeks straight. But now they were performing in an international competition.

"Come on, Miriam! Now's not the time to quit!"

Mei was determined. There was so much on the line: the contest judges were members of 4*Town themselves! The band had even performed at the finalists' reception. Mei could've sworn Robaire was looking right at their table!

4*Town was the reason the 4*Townies had gotten together. If the girls could show even half of what they were capable of, 4*Town would be blown away.

"We can do this!" Mei urged them.

"Okay, but my feet hurt—"

"Hold on, Mei!" Miriam said, looking over my shoulder. "How come *you're* the leader?" She frowned as she read over the story. "And why am I the one that's out of shape?"

Priya was lying on my bed. "This is *fan fiction*," she called out. "We can write anything we want."

"*Aaarggh!* Why are we arguing?" Abby fumed. "This is supposed to be *fun*!"

It had been precisely one year since the four of us had become the 4*Townies. For the grade seven talent show, Miriam and Priya had planned to dance to a 4*Town song. But the week of the show, two members of their group ate suspicious cafeteria nachos and came down with food poisoning. Abby and I loved 4*Town more than anything, so Miriam and Priya asked us to join. I really wanted to—I was already in the show as part of band—but I knew Mom would be in the audience and she wouldn't approve. So I helped out backstage with costumes instead. Our group won, and the rest, as they say, was 4*Townie history.

To celebrate our anniversary, we were writing a

fanfic tribute to our love of the greatest boy band of all time: 4*Town.

"I may not have started the 4*Townies, but I'm the one who leads us into battle." I jumped on my bed. "When the school wanted to play classical music in the halls before first bell, what did I say?"

"No way!" my friends exclaimed, looking up at me.

"That's right. I said we need music that speaks to us!"

"Preach!" Abby shouted.

"Who went down to the principal's office? Me. Who argued that 4*Town was the voice of our generation? Me." I raised my fist in the air. "I said, 'We don't want music that's been passed around like hand-me-down clothes. We want music that speaks to the kids of today! 4*Town is life! 4*Town is joy! 4*Town is *everything*!' "

"That took guts, Mei," noted Priya. "And a distinct lack of tact."

"Because of me, kids at our school hear the joyful sounds of 4*Town at the start of each day."

Miriam gave me a big grin. "That's our Mei. That's why we love her."

"We sure do!" said Abby.

I jumped off the bed, and the 4*Townies banded together for a big group hug. I might have been the leader, but there was no better group to lead.

"You guys are the best," I said.

Miriam, Priya, and Abby were my closest friends. We were like an atom: you couldn't split us up. But we had more in common than a love of boy bands. Like me, my friends wanted to make the world a better place. We were organizing a protest to save the environment, and the 4*Townies were at my place to make signs. Well, technically.

"I like that you already mention Robaire," said Miriam. "How about we make him a major character in the story?" Robaire was the coolest member of 4*Town.

"I agree. More Robaire, please," said Priya. She started playing with my little handheld game, which had a cute character that you took care of like a pet. I had named it Robaire Junior in honor of his greatness.

"What if Robaire has a record company?" Abby cried. "He needs to sign new bands and wants to sign us!"

Everyone loved it, and I wrote it all down. Pretty soon, the 4*Townies were done with the first chapter. I held out my hand and wiggled my fingers. My friends gathered around me and did the same.

"One . . . two . . . three . . ." I began.

*"4*Town forevah!"* we all shouted. *"Ride or die!"*

Miriam pulled out a 4*Town CD from her backpack, and we danced to the grooves of the best band in the world.

When the first song ended, Miriam flopped onto my bed. "Do you think Robaire is interested in brunettes?" She had a dreamy look on her face. "His last girlfriend was blond." Not surprisingly, Miriam was a brunette.

"I think it's safe to say he isn't interested in brunettes who are thirteen years old," replied Priya.

I checked the time. "Hey, guys, are you hungry?" I asked. "My mom left us some food."

It was only us in the house. Dad was out grocery shopping, and Mom was at a community event. She did stuff like that to show leadership. Her family was a big deal in the Chinese community. Mom's side came to Canada a long time ago and established the Lee Family Temple in the center of Chinatown. We lived next to the temple and took care of it to that day.

While my friends sat at the dining room table, I got the food ready. I left the kitchen carrying a big steaming platter. "Homemade dumplings," I announced. "They're *sooo* tasty!" My mouth watered as I set it on the table. I bet my friends had never eaten real Chinese dumplings before. They were little pillows of yumminess. "Guys, dig in!"

Abby grabbed one with chopsticks. "This is awesome!" she said, gobbling it up.

Priya didn't seem so sure. "What's in it?"

"Cabbage, carrots, tofu, ginger. They're vegetarian especially for you."

Priya took a bite. "Hey, this is really good!"

"Thanks! Mom and I made them."

Miriam scanned the living room. "Um, you and your mom are really tight, aren't you?"

"Yeah, sure. Why?"

"Oh, it's no big deal." She looked uncomfortable. She was staring at our family photos on the wall. "It's just that you seem to do everything together. Like . . . *everything.*"

I didn't know what she was talking about. The photos were pretty standard. There was me and Mom winning the mother-daughter badminton tournament, me and Mom doing mother-daughter spa day, me and Mom at the mother-daughter climb up the CN Tower, and me and Mom at Take Your Daughter to Work Day. That was kind of a nonevent, since Mom and I work at the temple already. But we wanted to celebrate, so we posed with our mother-daughter temple badges.

"Do you guys do anything that's not, like, the same?"

"Sure! It was my idea to spell 'TEAM LEE' on our badminton shirts in capital letters." That was a big deal!

Mom wanted to capitalize just the first letters, i.e. *Team Lee*. Yeah, right, like that would work.

Abby shrieked. "Whoa, is that you and your mom at Miracle Mart?" She was staring at the mantel.

"Yup, we go every year."

Her eyes bugged out.

Every Christmas, Mom and I took over Miracle Mart for our photo shoot. We didn't do the fake-Santa, fake-ugly-sweater thing. We wore traditional Chinese dresses called cheongsam. Mom brought her own decorations, and we posed with Mom smiling at me, and me kneeling in front of her, serving her tea.

"My mom's so cool," I told them. "The photographer wants us to say this cheesy Miracle Mart slogan, and Mom's like, 'No way I'm gonna do that.'"

My friends didn't say a word for like five minutes. Then Abby said quietly, "How long have you been doing this?"

"Since I was four. Every photo goes up on the mantel."

"Mei, I'm not sure how to tell you this," Priya began,

"but it's the same picture. The exact same. It's like you photocopied the original nine times and pasted in a bigger you."

I shrugged. "Doesn't everyone do that?"

The 4*Townies looked at each other. "Whoa, look at the time!" Abby cried. "I have to get home soon!"

We finished eating, and everyone grabbed their stuff and left.

They never did answer my question.

The next day, Mom and I went out for lunch at our favorite noodle house in Chinatown. We had done this every Sunday since I was little.

The restaurant was a couple of blocks from our house. It was sunny and beautiful that day, and the streets in Chinatown were busy. Well, they were always busy. That was why I loved it! There were workers carting supplies from huge trucks, seniors taking their daily walk, and families meeting up for dim sum. Malls were safe and boring, with elevator music playing in the background. Chinatown had streetcars clanging and people shouting in Cantonese across the street. My favorite was the produce stands. Old women with faces like wrinkled raisins set up on the sidewalk and sold bundles of bok choy and bags of oranges and pears to anyone passing by.

As Mom and I were walking, we heard a shout. "Mrs.

Lee! Mrs. Lee!" called a short woman at the herbalists' store. She rushed out into the street to greet us. The woman was Mrs. Chong from the local seniors' center. "I'm glad I saw you today. Good news—the city agreed to provide more funding. Thank you so much for petitioning on our behalf!"

Mom smiled and shook her hand, like the Queen accepting flowers. "It was no problem at all," she said. I'd seen her talk like this a thousand times to people. She was a bigwig in Chinatown. "The seniors' center plays a vital role in the community, and the Lee Family Temple will always stand by you. We love our seniors!"

Mrs. Chong's hand moved to her heart. "I can't thank you enough!"

"If the center needs anything, don't hesitate to ask." Mom nudged me forward. "This is my daughter, Mei-Mei."

"My goodness, you've grown, Mei-Mei!" Mrs. Chong exclaimed. She looked at Mom, her eyes shining. "Your mother is a wonderful person. I hope you know how lucky you are."

I said I did and nodded modestly. Well, I pretended to be modest. My mom was the best! Everyone knew that. I looked up at Mom and smiled. She smiled back and winked.

When we finally arrived at the noodle house, Mom immediately asked to speak to the manager. The man approached us nervously. "Hello, Mrs. Lee," he faltered. "How can I help you this time?"

Mom didn't mince words. "During our last visit, we had extremely slow service. Our server was tardy with the drinks and our main dishes. As frequent patrons, we expect a higher standard."

He wiped his face. "Of course. We have many fine servers here. Is there another one you prefer?" The servers saw us and cowered behind the restaurant counter.

Mom aimed her finger to the right. "That one!"

It was a young guy. He'd never served us before. He looked like he was going to have a heart attack.

"Good, right away, Mrs. Lee," the manager said, and looked at the young man, who was trying to flee into the kitchen.

Mom and I took our usual table by the window. She ordered a bowl of congee, which was Chinese rice porridge, and I got the noodle soup with duck. As the server left, Mom took a quick look in the mirror and smoothed out her hair. She was wearing a brocade jacket that day, with a silk scarf knotted around her neck. Some moms wouldn't care how they looked at a noodle house lunch. Not Mom. She never lowered her standards.

Finally, she turned to me. "Okay, Mei-Mei, let's hear it. Roll call."

"Come on, I told you everything." It was a game we always played.

"I'm sure there's more. Roll call!"

"Okay," I said, and got ready. "Mrs. Braude did an instrument grading the other day." Once a month, the music teacher made each student stand up and perform a solo. Then she ranked the students according to how well they performed. The student who played best in their section was named first chair and changed seats to the front. "I nailed my piece! And I moved up by four spots."

"It sounds a bit cutthroat for a music class," Mom mused. "But you seem to be managing."

It didn't bother me at all. "It's kinda fun, actually, like a cross between music class and boot camp. Only the strongest gets to be first chair."

She smiled at me. "And that's going to be you soon, right, Mei-Mei?"

"You bet!"

She gave me a high five. "Good work, kiddo! Those flute lessons are really paying off."

"Wait, there's more!" I added. This had been the best part of the class. "Tyler Nguyen-Baker played his trumpet solo so badly Mrs. Braude bumped him down by three chairs—and there are only four people in his section!"

The 4*Townies had laughed with me about it in the locker room later. Tyler always gave us such a hard time about liking 4*Town.

Mom looked satisfied. "That'll teach him. That boy has been a pest towards you since kindergarten. Don't ever let him push you around."

"He's so annoying! He called me an 'overachieving dork-narc.' That's not even a real word."

Tyler Nguyen-Baker was my archenemy, if such a thing existed at middle school. Tyler was so full of himself. He always had to have the latest video game, the most expensive sneakers. What he really had was the biggest head.

The server arrived at our table with our food. Spirals of steam floated up from the bowls. Mom spooned some congee into a small bowl for me, like she always did, and added a bit of soy sauce. "Here you are, Mei-Mei."

The congee came with a plate of youtiao on the side. Youtiao were long fried doughnuts you used for dipping. I stuck one end into the congee and took a big bite. It was heaven. The youtiao was hot, crispy, and chewy at the same time.

"How did the study session go?" Mom asked.

"Study session? Oh, you mean the protest meeting?" I said, taking another bite. "We're in good shape."

Mom raised her eyebrows. "A protest? You didn't tell me about that."

"Oh, I analyzed our past environmental protests and realized we didn't think big enough. If we want to make a difference, we have to shake up the school!" I took a sip of water. "Plus, ongoing extracurriculars is important for college applications. They want to see long-term involvement."

Mom smiled at me. "You're destined to be a leader, Mei-Mei. You're always three steps ahead!" Then she paused and added, "I do hope you managed to study for your math test, too."

"You bet! This unit is easy-peasy."

Mom looked relieved. "Good, I'm glad. That math teacher of yours isn't entirely behind you, you know," she said. Apparently, during the parent-teacher conference, Mr. Kieslowski described me as a "very enterprising young woman" as well as "mildly annoying."

"You can't take Mr. K seriously. He's our gym teacher,

too. Really, Mom! He thinks that zero can be divided by any number, *including* zero!"

"For Pete's sake!" Mom exclaimed. "They let anyone teach math these days." She shook her head. "I'll have to speak to the principal about that." Mom had been a Mathlete and the high school Math Olympics champ. She knew the score.

She eyed me suspiciously. "Was Miriam at the house yesterday?"

"For sure! She's great at problem-solving."

Mom nodded. "Good, so long as she is focusing on schoolwork."

She didn't like Miriam. The last time Mom met her at a school event, Miriam had just run into Matthew Soto, the cutest boy in our grade. Miriam had babbled for like ten minutes about how hot he was. My mother was not impressed. Since then, Mom had pegged her as a bad influence, which wasn't fair, because Miriam was one of the nicest people I knew.

"I don't want you growing up too fast in the wrong ways." Mom seemed nervous and poured herself some tea.

"Things are great, Mom! You don't have to worry," I said. The 4*Townies were the best. She just had to get to know them better. "I want to show my friends around the temple. They'll love it! Can they come on a tour this week?"

Her eyes lit up. "That sounds wonderful. Of course they can! Why not bring them on Wednesday? We don't have any other groups booked then." She relaxed a bit and smiled.

There was a knocking sound on the restaurant window. We turned around and saw a gaggle of Chinese women carrying groceries, pressing their nostrils against the pane of glass. They were waving frantically, like getting our attention was an Olympic sport.

"Ming, good to see you!" one of them called out. Another woman brought her hand to her face like a telephone receiver. *Call me,* she mouthed.

My mom was such a rock star.

Soon the server passed by. Mom flagged him down and asked for a few orders of sticky rice in lotus leaf to go. "It's for your dad," she said to me. "They're not as good as the ones he makes, but he'll like them."

Dad was a connoisseur of dim sum food and an amazing cook. Mom liked to say that the best Chinese restaurant in Toronto was our kitchen.

"By the way, I need your help this afternoon at the temple," she added. "New shipments of souvenirs arrived on Friday, and we have to set them up at the gift shop." *Ooh! Temple souvenirs!* They were so fun, especially the coloring books.

"The seniors are starting tai chi again this week. Now that the weather's nicer, there will be more people practicing in the courtyard." She snapped her fingers. "Oh! Mr. Gao wants your locker combination."

"Huh, why would he want that?" Mr. Gao was always doing random stuff. All he could steal from my locker were textbooks and 4*Town posters.

Mom rolled her eyes. "It's for his lottery ticket. He needs more numbers for this week's draw. He thinks it's his destiny to win someday. Mr. Gao's a sweet old man. Humor him, Mei-Mei."

"I'll tell him at our next chess game." Mr. Gao was one of the seniors who hung around the temple. He was also my favorite chess opponent.

As we were finishing our meal, I thought back to the visit with the 4*Townies the day before. "Mom, when my friends were over, they noticed all the photos of you and me at the house. . . ."

She looked at me. "Yes?"

I wasn't sure how to put this. "It seemed a little strange to them."

"How so?"

"They wouldn't say."

Mom tensed up. "I see," she said with a frosty edge to her voice. She took out a pocket mirror and checked her makeup. "You know what, Mei-Mei? Some people in this world are jealous. They can't be happy if someone else has something they don't have." She fixed her hair and scarf again. "Some children aren't close to their parents the way we are. No matter. Don't let them get to you. Be proud of who you are, Mei-Mei. Who *we* are."

That made sense. Mom and I were a team. Not everyone was like that.

She held out her hand. "And who are we, kiddo?"

"We're Team Lee!" I answered, and gave her a high five.

"That's my girl!"

The server finally arrived with our takeout in a white plastic bag. Mom picked up our order and turned to him before we left. "I hope you weren't expecting a tip from us today," she sniffed. "We waited forever for our food."

It was the final dress rehearsal before the big performance. The 4*Townies sang and danced their hearts out onstage.

Everyone in the auditorium stopped to watch. "We don't stand a chance of winning," groaned the band from Sweden.

At the back of the auditorium stood a new security guard. He tried to stay hidden. Even though he wore a disguise of a uniform and sunglasses, it could be only one person: Robaire. Rumor had it that Robaire was starting his own record label and was traveling undercover, checking out different bands to sign. People said Robaire had shown up at different rehearsals dressed as a dentist, a cowboy, and even a pizza deliveryman.

These girls are incredible! Robaire thought as he watched the 4*Townies perform. I knew it the moment I first saw them. He knew the girls were going to be stars, but one person stood out in his mind: the girl with the green tuque. She had awesome moves. Her name was MIRIAM.

"Excuse me?" Abby cried, furious. "The story is supposed to be about all of us!"

Miriam held out the notebook. "It is! Besides, he can't always look at all of us at the same time, right?" It had been Miriam's turn to write the next section, and—surprise, surprise—the story ended up being about her and Robaire.

The 4*Townies were gathered in the temple courtyard that afternoon. My friends were there for a tour . . . well, eventually.

"When we started, we agreed that we'd take turns writing," I argued. "It's Miriam's turn, and she's free to write the way she wants. She still mentions the 4*Townies and says we're great. I say we let Miriam's section stand!"

One by one, Abby and Priya agreed. Miriam put her arm around my shoulder. "Thanks, Mei. You're the best." She gave me a big smile, flashing me a view of her new braces. "Hey, I've got an idea!" she blurted out. "Bands do videos for their songs. Why don't we do one, too?"

"That would be awesome!" Abby shouted. "We can get a videocam and record a dance routine."

"I'm in! My dad has one. I can borrow his," I said. "We should dress up in 4*Townie costumes."

Priya had a flash of brilliance. "Don't famous groups have their own tour merchandise? Like T-shirts and hats?"

"We can get 4*Townie posters!"

"And key chains!"

Suddenly, I heard the click of high heels. My heart seized up. It was Mom.

"Miriam, put the story away!" I whispered. I grabbed her knapsack and handed it to her. "Hide it—now!"

Miriam looked stunned. "What?"

Mom greeted us with a smile. "Good afternoon, girls. Lovely to see you here." Luckily, Priya had managed to stuff the notebook into Miriam's backpack. "Mei-Mei tells me you're interested in the temple. That is wonderful," Mom said, and eyed each of my friends closely.

"I'm so excited! This is awesome, Mrs. Lee," said Abby.

"The temple is so beautiful," added Priya.

Mom put her hand on my shoulder. "Mei-Mei, unfortunately, the Business Improvement Association is meeting tonight. I won't be able to lead the tour with you."

"But what about the Sun Yee play?" I whined.

Mom sighed. "I'm sorry, Mei-Mei. You'll have to do the tour without it." *But the play is the best part,* I thought. Mom turned to my friends. "I hope you girls enjoy the temple, but please don't stay too late. I don't want you taking the streetcar—"

Miriam snapped her fingers. "Hey, Mei, guess who I saw on the streetcar on the way over?" She nudged me. "Devon!"

Mom stared at her, alarmed. "Devon? Who's Devon?" she asked. "Mei-Mei, you've never mentioned this boy before."

"It's no one special," I said quickly. "Mir's really friendly. She always talks to, like, random people on the streetcar." I watched Mom sigh in relief. Meanwhile, Miriam looked at me, confused.

Right then, I saw Mr. Gao crossing the courtyard, and I waved to him like crazy. "Mr. Gao, did you get your lottery ticket?" I shouted.

He beamed and held up a ticket, which fluttered in the breeze. "The fates are on my side!" he called out. He strolled through the courtyard and greeted the other seniors.

I saw my chance. "Okay, guys, time for the tour!" I shouted. I turned and waved goodbye to Mom on the steps.

"That was close," I muttered as I led my friends back to the entrance. "Mir, you can't talk about boys in front of my mom. I don't want to get her upset."

"You mean Devon?" she asked, puzzled. "Why can't I talk about him? He's really cute! Next time we go to Daisy Mart, I'll point him out to you." She gave me a wink.

Miriam was nice and all, but sometimes she just didn't get it.

We went outside to the entrance steps, where two red panda statues guarded the front gates. My parents let me name them when I was four. I chose Bart and Lisa.

I loved the temple. It was right in the middle of Chinatown. You could see the CN Tower and the Toronto skyline in the distance. But once you stepped through the gates, you were in another world. The sky was clear that day, and there was a breeze blowing. It was the perfect day for a tour. Miriam, Abby, and Priya waited for me to begin.

"Here we are at the entrance to the Lee Family Temple." I pointed to my badge. "I am Meilin Lee, assistant temple keeper, your host for today's tour."

The 4*Townies broke into applause. Abby gave a whoop. "You go, Mei!"

"The Lee Family Temple is the oldest temple in Toronto. It was established to honor the Lee ancestors and has been in my family for generations. It is my privilege to show you the temple and its traditions. Please follow me."

I proudly led them across the courtyard, past a group of seniors doing tai chi. "The temple was built according to the traditional temples in China." I pointed up. "The temple roof is made of tile and curves like the roofs of a pagoda."

Priya gazed up. "That's so cool!" she murmured.

"A temple courtyard has to have elements of nature," I continued. "Ours has an outdoor pond filled with koi fish."

Abby loved animals. She bent down to the silver and orange fish and waved hello as we went by. I saw Mr. Gao, contemplating his next move, at the marble chess table in the corner.

My friends listened to every word of my guide talk, and I couldn't have been happier. I couldn't believe the 4*Townies were here, in my world! The temple was truly my home.

We arrived at the entrance of the main hall. I checked inside. The dark hall was thick with the smell of cedar and burning incense. The 4*Townies huddled around me and peered in.

Miriam's mouth dropped. "O.M.G."

Rows of red paper lanterns hung from the ceiling. To the left was a small nook where incense coils dangled from above. The room shimmered from the glow of lit candles. In the middle of the hall was the centerpiece: a large tapestry of a Chinese woman in flowing robes. She was flanked by tapestries of red pandas. Incense, candles, and plates of fruit lay on an altar in her honor.

"This altar is dedicated to one of our most revered ancestors. To this day, she is honored in the Lee family." I turned to my friends. "My fellow 4*Townies, I am proud to be a direct descendant of the original trailblazer of the Lee family: Sun Yee."

Sun Yee hovered in the air. She was dressed simply, with her hands tucked inside her robes. There wasn't anything fancy about her: she wore her hair in a bun, and her headpiece was a plain gold band. But Sun Yee had a serene smile on her face, like the problems of us mortals didn't bother her anymore.

Miriam went up to the tapestry. "Wow, you're really related to her?" She studied it closely. "That's pretty rad."

I had heard Sun Yee stories my entire life. It was like she was a living relative. "Yeah, Sun Yee was awesome! She loved animals and defended them. Imagine doing that in ancient China—she stood up for animal rights."

"So you two are kinda the same! You love animals, too," Abby said.

"And you're trying to protect them through environmental action," Priya noted.

I hadn't thought about that before. That was really cool. Sun Yee had courage and character. My mom liked to say they were traits that ran in the family. Maybe my love of nature came from her, too.

"Sun Yee loved all animals, but she loved the red panda in particular," I said, pointing out the pandas on either side of her. There were red pandas all over the temple. Red panda carvings decorated the hall, red panda statues were on the roof, and Bart and Lisa stood at the front gates.

Priya noticed the objects on the altar. "Mei, what are these things? They have the red panda symbol, too." She was about to pick one up.

"No!" I yelled. Her hand stopped in midair. "My mom freaks out if anyone touches these things. They've been in our family forever," I explained, pulling her away. Mom was super careful inside the main hall. She always told me it was the heart of the temple and the Lee family.

Then I had an amazing idea. The temple had other cool

stuff, and my friends could goof around all they wanted. "You wanna see the gift shop?"

The 4*Townies gasped. "Are you kidding? Of course!"

As veterans of the Toronto District School Board field trips, we knew that the best part of any visit was the gift shop.

Luckily, ours was awesome.

"This is awesome!" cried Abby, peeking through a red panda mask. "Do I look like a real panda? *Grrrrr!*"

Priya checked out a red panda T-shirt. "Yes, I'm frightened for my life. Everyone, run," she said, searching for its price tag.

"This is so cool!" Miriam squeezed my arm. "Is there any Sun Yee stuff?"

"Over there, in the corner," I said. "We've got coloring books about Sun Yee, too." I had loved those books as a kid. That was where I'd gotten my love of drawing.

The gift shop had cool stuff like panda figurines and red envelopes for Lunar New Year. My friends could've stayed forever, but Mom soon appeared at the doorway. She tapped her watch, and I nodded. It was time for them to go.

My friends got their stuff together and got ready to leave. *Sigh.* It was nice having them there. They thanked my mom on the way out, and we walked back to noisy Spadina Avenue. A taxi had plowed into the back of a vegetable truck, and the owners were screaming at each other in the middle of the road. Cars were honking from every direction. We were back in Toronto.

"Thanks for coming, guys! And thanks for being nice to my mom. She's always afraid I'm hanging around 'head-bangers.' Too bad you can't stay longer, but she doesn't want you going home in the dark."

Priya looked at the sky. "Uh, Mei, it's still light out. It won't be dark for another three hours."

"But you're taking public transit. It's totally different."

They still seemed confused.

"You have to come again," I said. "You haven't seen the best part! Mom and I do a two-person play with Sun Yee and the red panda."

My friends got quiet and glanced at each other.

"What's up? Something wrong?"

"No, nothing," said Miriam. She gave me a shoulder hug. "We just noticed that your mom likes to hang around you a lot. That's all."

Abby jumped in. "It's no big deal, Mei! I get it—my folks are Korean. They tell me what to do, too. It's all about honoring your parents." Her face turned red, and she shook her fists. "It gets me so angry sometimes!"

What were they talking about? "Guys, I honor my parents by honoring myself!"

Abby turned to look at the cabbage from the truck. Priya picked at her fingernails. Miriam coughed.

"I mean . . . I have responsibilities. I'm cool with that. It's not all about me, y'know?" They didn't understand that I had the best of both worlds. "I've got you guys and school, and I've got Mom and the temple. Two halves make a whole, right?"

My friends stared down, like their feet were the most interesting things on the planet. Time to show some Mei swagger!

I stepped into the middle of the sidewalk. "My fellow 4*Townies, ever since I turned thirteen, I've been doing my own thing, makin' my own moves twenty-four seven, three hundred sixty-five!" The owner of the barbecue shop waved to me from his window.

"I wear what I want, say what I want, and will not hesitate to do a spontaneous cartwheel if so moved!" I checked for sharp objects, then placed my hands on the ground and kicked up my legs. Gymnastics was my best activity in elementary school phys ed!

"Oh, no, Mei, not here!" Miriam wailed.

Abby cried, "I don't have any more bandages!"

I was fully upside down when I felt a rush of blood to my brain. The streets of Chinatown swam before me as I toppled to the ground. The 4*Townies gasped and hurried to my rescue.

Priya helped me up. "What did I say, Mei? If you're going to do this, you have to wear a helmet!"

I dusted myself off. "Thanks, I'm all good!" I picked up my backpack. "Practice makes perfect, right?"

The Spadina streetcar finally arrived. We had one last group hug. "Don't forget about the protest. Abby, you got the secret weapon?"

She nodded. "I'll get them from the cafeteria tomorrow!"

The 4*Townies went to the back window and waved to me. I smiled and waved back. I watched them leave for the station. For some reason, they seemed to be shaking their heads at me.

"Guys, are you ready?"

Mei looked at the other 4*Townies backstage. Her heart pounded. The 4*Townies were the last ones to perform. All the other groups had played. There had been bands from France, Singapore, Brazil, and even Iceland. They were all amazing. The 4*Townies had to be better than good to win. They had to be unbelievable.

Mei peeked from behind the curtain. Robaire, Jesse, Tae Young, Aaron T, and Aaron Z sat right next to the edge of the stage. The guys looked every inch like superstars. Mei could hardly believe this was all happening. The show was being broadcast on TV. She could hear the audience murmuring.

Abby had done the group's makeup. She checked everyone and gave a thumbs-up. Priya did a last-minute check of their costumes. Miriam adjusted her tuque.

The announcer came on. "For our final performance, from Toronto, Canada . . . the 4*Townies!"

Mei raised her fist in the air. "Let's do this!"

I burst through the front doors of my school, clutching my flute. *Aagh!* I was late for the protest! I'd been having nightmares lately and slept through my alarm. Miriam was at her locker, munching on potato chips (her favorite guilty breakfast). Priya was deep into the latest vampire-teen-supernatural-action-fantasy novel. Abby was already in environmental action mode: she was telling off some grade seven students for littering in the hallway. She was so mad she started swearing in Korean.

"Sorry I'm late," I gasped. I reached into my locker and pulled out the megaphone I'd borrowed from Mr. K. I had told him we needed it for a play. The other 4*Townies gathered around me, signs in hand.

"Are you ready to change the world?" I asked.

"So ready," chimed in Miriam.

"I was born to do this," said Priya.

Abby appeared, fresh from her tirade. *"Let's burn this place to the ground!"*

We took our protest gear and, together, marched down the main corridor of Lester B. Pearson Middle School.

"Wake up, LBP Middle School! It's 2002 and our cafeteria is still using plastic cups!" I roared.

Students filed past us down the hall. None gave us a second look.

"Preach, sister! That's right!" called out Miriam.

"Plastic kills," added Priya.

Abby thumped the drum she had borrowed from her brother.

The 4*Townies had organized protests before. For our last one, we had set up a table in front of the cafeteria with a petition to save the old-growth forests. All kids did was leave their empty juice boxes on our table. One student asked if it was a lunchtime detention.

The fate of our planet was at stake. We realized we had to disrupt the social order. We needed to do something gutsy, something daring. Something dangerous.

"4*Townies, get out the secret weapon," I whispered. My friends nodded.

"The ocean is dying!" I bellowed. Then we all whipped out packets of cafeteria ketchup, ripped them open, and smeared the oozy redness over ourselves. "The cafeteria has blood on their hands!"

The 4*Townies fell to the floor, fainting at man's destruction of nature. We were environmental roadkill.

Then the bell rang.

Two kids stepped over us. "What do you think's going to be on the test today? I studied so hard," one said.

A boy raced down the hall. "C'mon! I hear we got a sub. Ms. Neely's out again."

Kids wandered past us to their homerooms, oblivious to the environmental crisis that loomed in front of them.

I brought the megaphone to my lips one last time. "Power to the people!" I cried. Then I muttered under my breath, "Kids our age suck."

"Preach," said Priya, oozing ketchup from her nostrils.

The school caretaker appeared and looked at the four of us on the ground. He leaned against his mop and shook his head. "I hope you don't expect me to clean this up."

I gotta admit the response to our protest was disappointing.

Mr. K had asked for the megaphone back. He said I couldn't borrow school gym equipment from him again. The 4*Townies were temporarily banned from using cafeteria condiments.

"That was the lamest thing I've ever seen!" sneered Tyler. "Who cares about a bunch of dolphins, anyway?"

I lost my temper. "Oh, yeah, Tyler? Wait until the ozone layer disappears!"

"Global warming is real!" cried Abby.

"It's all baloney," he said. He was wearing a pair of shiny new sneakers that morning. "Only someone who's dumb enough to like 4*Town would believe it."

"He just dissed the Great Ones!" Abby fumed. "Let me at him!" She charged, ready to throttle him.

"Whoa, girl, he's not worth it!" Miriam hissed as the 4*Townies pulled her back.

Who cared what stupid-evil Tyler thought? He'd been a creep ever since we were little.

"Come on, guys!" I called out. Together we marched to our first class. "We're not going to let a scrawny runt like Tyler ruin our day. Or our planet."

Luckily, my favorite class was next: math. Well, every class was my favorite. There wasn't a single class where I wasn't crushing it. In the afternoon, we had French, and I gave a flawless presentation about the history of Bordeaux. By then, the 4*Townies had entirely forgotten about Tyler Nguyen-Baker.

But I hadn't forgotten about the environment. I was already thinking about our next protest. This was going to be a long fight. I was more than ready!

When school ended, Miriam came up to my locker. "We've got a surprise for you," she said.

"You're gonna love it," added Priya. "Meet us outside."

The 4*Townies waited while I went to the office. I had been trying to convince the school secretary to purchase paper made from alternative fibers. "There's eco-friendly paper made with bamboo or even leftover harvested sugarcane," I argued. "Trees don't have to die just for our worksheets!"

I checked the time and realized I had to go. (Mrs. Jagaric looked relieved.) I promised Mom I would help clean the temple. It was a huge job, and we always did it together. I grabbed my stuff and hurried outside.

"Hey, Mei, we're over here!" yelled Abby. "Where are you going?"

"I have to head to the temple!"

My friends caught up to me. "You're not leaving, young lady," Priya said, and crossed her arms.

Miriam put her hand on my shoulder. "He's there today." She broke into a huge grin. "You're finally going to see *him*."

My friends crept up to the Daisy Mart convenience store like middle school panthers stalking prey.

"What's so special about this guy, anyhow?" I asked. For the past week, Miriam, Abby, and Priya couldn't stop talking about him.

"Shhh!" Abby hissed. She motioned to me. "Come on, get your butt over here!"

My friends hid under the store window, giggling. I crawled down, too. A man with a huge golden retriever walked by, and the dog sniffed my earlobes. *Ugh!* I wished my friends would hurry up. I couldn't stay there all day.

One by one, they popped their heads up. They peered in, mesmerized, like there was a life-sized chocolate sundae in the window.

"Ohhh . . ." they sighed.

"Mei, come have a look. It's Devon," whispered Miriam.

Finally, I had a peek. Devon was the store clerk. He must've been about seventeen. I took another look, and then another. *Uh, this is the guy they've been swooning over? Really?*

"My mom cuts his hair at the salon," Abby sighed. "I've felt it—it's very soft!" Priya and Miriam asked if they could have some.

This is so embarrassing, I thought. *I need new friends.*

There was nothing special about him. He had brown hair and was kinda scruffy. He wore a bucket hat that covered his eyes. I'd seen panhandlers who dressed better.

I reached into my backpack for my *Tween Beat* magazine. "May I remind you what real men look like?" I pulled it out and showed them the cover. It was a special issue about 4*Town.

Now this was a group that was swoonworthy. They were more than pretty faces in a boy band: Jesse went to art school. Tae Young fostered injured doves. Robaire spoke French (*Oui! Oui!*). And Aaron T and Aaron Z were really talented, too. I was sure they were great at lots of stuff.

I could picture Jesse at a potter's wheel, making wonderful things out of clay. Or Tae Young nurturing a hurt bird. Or Robaire at an outdoor cafe near the Eiffel Tower, ordering food in French, while Aaron T and Aaron Z were doing . . . Well, whatever it was, it must have been pretty great, too.

I had a favorite daydream: Me and the members of 4*Town stood on top of a mountain, just like in the video for "Break Free," their anthem song. The camera panned from above as the boys gazed at the sky. The wind whipped around us fiercely, but not fiercely enough to muss our hair. At the very top of the peak, there I was, Meilin Lee, my hands reaching out to the heavens.

Break free, be who you wanna be.
Your soul can touch the sky,
Oh my, oh my . . .

"We are 4*Townies, remember? Ride or die!" I declared.

Priya looked at me, unimpressed. "Tickets to 4*Town are like a bajillion dollars." She pointed behind her, at the window. "And Devon's right here."

"And free!" Abby added.

Thanks, way to destroy my dream.

All of a sudden, I saw the streetcar coming and remembered I was late. "I gotta go—"

"Wait, we're going karaokeing today!" Miriam said.

Ooh, I love karaoke! But Mom is waiting for me. Aargh . . .

The 4*Townies huddled in front of me, making sad puppy-dog faces. "Pleeeease?" begged Priya.

"I can't!" I finally said. "It's cleaning day!"

Miriam sighed. "Every day is cleaning day. Can't you just get one afternoon off?"

"But I like cleaning," I said. They didn't seem to understand. "Plus, I got this new feather duster, and oh my gosh, you guys, it picks up so much dirt. It's bananas!"

Miriam stepped in front of me and held out her hand.

"Fine, I'll let you go if you can pass . . . the gauntlet!" There was a big smile on her face.

Oh, no, Mir, not here, out in public . . .

Abby covered her mouth with her hands and began beatboxing. She sounded like a garden hose that had sprung a leak. Then Priya joined in. Miriam bumped me with her hip and winked. "You know you can't resist it!" she said, and started singing and dancing to 4*Town's "Nobody Like You."

It was the song the 4*Townies had performed a year earlier, for the school talent contest we won. Well, the three of them won. But I'd joined in ever since. I couldn't help it. That was the song that had brought us all together.

Miriam, Abby, and Priya were already singing and dancing, in full view of everyone. The streetcar driver kept the doors open and watched us from a distance. So I put down my backpack and joined my friends for a few minutes of silliness and fun.

When we finished, the 4*Townies all cheered. "See? That was good," Miriam said, laughing. "You passed.

And here's your reward." She presented me with a CD of 4*Town's 1999 Australian tour, which she had made especially for me.

"OMG, Mir. I'll guard it with my life." I kissed it and said thank you about a thousand times. I held out my hand and wiggled my fingers. The others gathered around. "4*Town forevah!" we all shouted.

Now it was time to go. I hurried into the streetcar, promising to do karaoke next time with them. I told them I'd have time for sure. I didn't always have to be at the temple. Mom would understand.

As the streetcar pulled away, I went to the back window and waved to my friends. They were all staring at me. Again, they were shaking their heads.

The streetcar took forever to get home. I decided to get off a few stops early and run to the temple. "Crud, crud, crud," I huffed. I raced past the Chinatown markets and shops. They were busy, too, and I almost knocked over a man carrying a box of pastries.

"*Ai-ya!*" he shouted, and shook his fist at me.

As I rounded the corner, Bart and Lisa came into view. I was almost there.

There weren't a lot of seniors in the courtyard that day. "Hello, Meilin!" called out Mrs. Gao. Her husband was next to her, deep into his chess game.

"Still down for a rematch, Mr. Gao?"

"Bring it, Lee!" he said, and laughed.

I rushed to the gift shop and put on my badge, then did a quick bow in the ancestors' hall. Finally, I made it to the main temple and stepped through the doorway.

Mom was kneeling at the altar. She turned around

as soon as I walked in. "Mei-Mei, there you are!" she cried. "What happened?" (For the record, I was late by ten minutes.) She studied my face and grilled me. "Are you hurt? Are you hungry?" She had a plate of custard buns and shoved one into my mouth.

I'd been afraid this would happen. I knew she'd get upset if I was late.

"How was school today?" she asked.

"Killed it, per usual," I said. "Check it out!" I showed her the tests I'd gotten back that day.

Mom was so proud. "That's my little scholar!" She always said I could do anything I wanted.

I finished eating and went to kneel by the altar. Mom and I always paid our respects to our ancestors when I got home. We both lowered our heads, and Mom thanked Sun Yee for looking out for the family. "Especially Mei-Mei," she added, and looked at me warmly.

I smiled. "May we continue to serve and honor you and this community . . ."

"Always," we said in unison.

The hall flickered with the dim light of the altar candles. We bowed together.

This was home.

We did the daily temple briefing at Mom's desk. She studied her daybook like a general studying a battlefield.

"We have two tour groups coming today," she announced.

"Check," I said. "We'll reenact *Sun Yee and the Red Panda*. There's fresh duct tape on the panda costume."

She crossed it off her list. "The donation box?"

"Emptied and ready for the next group."

"Cleaning equipment?"

"New feather dusters tried and tested."

"Good! Next: gift shop."

"Souvenirs unpacked and displayed."

"The new red panda books?"

"On the shelves in alphabetical order," I said proudly.

"Lastly, the group is from Texas."

In my best official voice, I said, "The temple gift shop accepts Canadian money only."

Mom high-fived me. "That's my girl!"

The tours went really well that day. The visitors loved the play. One said it was the highlight of the tour. Mom pretended to be Sun Yee, and I was the red panda she cared for. It had always been fun to do—I had foam fingers for paws!—but I'd been doing it since I was four, so my costume was a bit ratty.

There was one thing that got me mad, though. It happened while we were cleaning. Mom and I were at the front gates when we saw these dumb teenagers spraying graffiti on the temple walls. Mom and I chased them off, but still, we had to clean up their mess.

I kept thinking about what had happened. When I was putting away the tour stuff, my mind went back to those boys. This place was special! I fumed. It had been in my family for generations. We worked hard to maintain it. And those jerks dissed the temple like it was a big joke. Good thing Mom told them off. She said she'd call their mothers—and she did! They didn't get away with it. But I could still hear them in my head, laughing at us, at our culture.

At that moment, I was in the main hall. I looked at the tapestry with Sun Yee's portrait. She deserved more respect than that. *Sun Yee was a fighter. She wouldn't have put up with those creeps.*

I paced around the altar, getting madder by the minute. Those boys weren't the only jerks around. There was also Tyler Nguyen-Baker at school. *He's one of them. He made fun of us after the protest. It's people like him who are destroying the environ—*

Suddenly, the air turned cold. I felt a chill along my arms. I looked around. There was no one in the hall except me. I went to the altar again. This time the candles went out. "Hello?" I said. My voice echoed in the hall.

That's strange, I thought. I could've sworn someone had come in. But the hall was empty. I looked outside, and there was no one in the courtyard. It was deserted. I shook it off. *Oh, well. Whatever.* It was dinnertime, and I was getting hungry. Plus, my favorite program, *Jade Palace Diaries*, was on that night! I lit the candles again and hurried home.

As soon as I walked into the house, I heard the hiss of water hitting a hot wok and rapid-fire chopping on a cutting board: Dad was cooking.

"I'm home!" I gave my father a hug. "What's for dinner?"

He wiped the wok's steam from his glasses. "Braised pork belly with steamed gai lan and oyster sauce." Dad shook the huge pan with his hand, making the food do somersaults in the air. "You like?"

"Are you kidding? *I love!*" I replied.

But he already knew that. He kissed me on the forehead. Braised pork belly was my favorite dish. Well, they all were. Dad was an awesome cook. Mom was in charge of the temple, but my father owned the kitchen.

"Mei-Mei, put your things away," Mom called out from the couch. "The show's started."

Mom and I were die-hard fans of *Jade Palace Diaries*,

a long-running Cantonese drama set in historical China. It had deception, murder, and devious characters who would stick a cleaver in their own amah's back. North American soap operas had nothing on *Jade Palace Diaries*.

Mom liked to fold dumplings while we watched, and she was already halfway through a batch. She patted the couch. "Come and sit," she said. "Sui Jyu is about to declare her undying love."

I took a wrapper and reached for some filling. "Hei Nin is so dense. He's like the dude on reality dating shows who can't tell which girl is mean and which one's nice."

Just as I said that, the characters embraced. Then the camera zoomed in on Sui Jyu, who had a sly look on her face.

"He should have listened to his mother and married Ling-Yi," said Mom.

The rich smell of roasted pork reached us in the living room. I took a deep breath and filled up my lungs. If someone could bottle that smell, I would use it as moisturizer, body wash, and acne cleanser.

I glanced back at the kitchen. Dad was busy cooking, doing his own thing. He wasn't like Mom. They were complete opposites. He was quiet and gentle and didn't like being the center of attention. At one point, I thought of him as a human coat rack, because all he did was hold Mom's purse at events while she made the speeches.

Then I realized that he was just different from her; that was all. He was a doer, not a talker. Mostly he showed his love by cooking for us. He made, like, epic amounts of food. He was the one who had taught me how to make dumplings, not Mom. My mother and I were close, but sometimes it was nice to be with someone who loved you but never said it out loud because he didn't have to. You just knew.

Mom and I finished the dumplings, and I brought the tray to the kitchen. Dad stopped to inspect them. He was really old-school about dumplings and liked to do a quality control check.

"Mmmm . . ." he mused, looking them over. He studied the pleats on each one, making sure each dumpling was tightly closed. "Mmm," he said again. Finally, he looked up from the tray. "Hm! Perfect."

"Yes!" It felt like I'd scored a winning goal.

I heard the TV show cut to a commercial break. An announcer came on as a 4*Town song played in the background. "The worldwide pop sensation 4*Town will be kicking off their North American tour! Tickets on sale now!"

My knees buckled and I gasped. I whipped around to watch the commercial.

Mom made a sour face. "Who are these . . . hip-hoppers? And why are they called 4*Town if there are five of them?"

Mom would freak out if she knew I was a 4*Townie. I straightened up and acted real casual. "I dunno," I said lightly. "Some of the kids at school like 'em. . . ."

She raised an eyebrow. "You mean Miriam? That girl is . . . odd."

I knew what Mom meant. When it came to boys,

Miriam just couldn't shut up. Talking like that in front of my mother was like waving a red flag in front of a bull.

Dad came out and told us dinner was ready. I took one last look at the ad. It would be incredible to see 4*Town live—and with the other 4*Townies, too!

I joined my folks at the table, but I wasn't hungry anymore. Who cared about pork belly? Seeing 4*Town live with my friends would be a once-in-a-lifetime experience. There was now something I craved more than Dad's food.

The 4*Townies did it! They won! They were the best in the world! The audience went wild with applause. The 4*Town judges stood up and gave them a standing ovation.

"You totally deserve it," said Robaire into his microphone. "There were a lot of talented groups, but you guys were phenomenal."

The 4*Townies looked at each other onstage and couldn't believe it. They had worked so hard for this, and their dreams had finally come true.

Meanwhile, Robaire had special plans for the 4*Townies. Their performance had confirmed his suspicions: they could be the best girl band ever!

The moment dinner was over, I had rushed to my room to write the next section of the fanfic. The news about the tour was amazing. *Imagine if 4*Town came to Toronto. That would be a dream come true.* I had badly wanted to call Miriam and tell her about the tour, but there was no way I could do that. Mom would hear, and I'd get in trouble. And Miriam would be banned from my house for life.

I glanced at the clock. I wasn't finished writing yet, but it was already six-thirty. I had to get started on my homework. Mr. K had assigned a lot. I put the fanfic notebook away in my backpack. I sighed and gave it a final pat. "I'll see you tomorrow," I promised.

I put on my headphones and got started on quadratic equations. The questions were easy, though, and my mind wandered within minutes. "I don't know why my friends dragged me to Daisy Mart," I grumbled. "Compared to 4*Town, Devon is a total dud."

I began doodling in the margins of my notes. *I mean, what does Devon have in common with 4*Town?* I thought. *They have hair. They have eyes. They're dudes. That's all.* I started a new drawing on the next page. Did Devon even have eyes? I couldn't see past that giant hat he had on.

The CD played "Let Your Dreams Fly" next, and I hummed along. It was the only song where Tae Young sang the lead. It was so soulful. Apparently, the song was inspired by his volunteer work with injured birds. TY's goal was to become a veterinarian someday. I stopped doing math and got lost in daydreaming. If only I could meet a guy like that.

The video for the song was amazing. The final scene had TY standing in the sun, and the bird he had cared for flew back and landed on his hand. I decided that would be my next picture. I sharpened my pencil and drew an outline of TY's face and body and then the bird.

After a few minutes, I stopped. "Whoa, what happened?" I blurted out. The face I had drawn wasn't Tae Young's. The figure was also wearing a big hat. "Hm . . . kinda looks like . . . Devon."

Hey, did I just draw the shabby guy from Daisy Mart?

I looked closely at my drawing. *Maybe Devon isn't that*

bad, I thought. I shaded in the features. He had nice hair, I remembered, and nice shoulders, too. *Devon isn't good-looking in an obvious way,* I thought. *His looks kinda sneak up on you.*

I kept on sketching. It was a hobby from when I was a kid. I used to trace the red pandas from the gift shop books. Later on, I spent hours drawing mythical creatures from fairy tales.

I had completely put aside math by then. There was too much swirling around in my head. I decided next to do a mermaid, my favorite thing to draw. On a fresh page, I sketched the outline of a mermaid perched on a rock. It looked pretty good, so I added details. I drew in the hat and face, and then I added scales to his tail. *Wait—his tail?*

I looked down at the merman's face. My throat got dry. *I just drew Devon again!*

There he was, looking up at me from the rock: Devon from Daisy Mart.

"What am I doing?" I blurted out. I flipped through my notebook. "I don't draw these kinds of things." But I did. I looked at the merman drawing again. *Actually, he's pretty cute,* I thought. Maybe my friends were right.

But I had to get back to work. There was a bunch of math to do. I'd think about Devon later, I decided. I went back to my textbook and searched for the next question. *To solve the equation, we have to find the meaning of X when X equals Devon.*

Whoa!

I glanced around me. *Hmmm . . . I can always finish up later,* I thought. *I mean, the unit is easy, and I can do the rest in the morning.* I took the notebook from my desk and strolled to my bed—ya know, to take a break.

I spread out the drawing and leaned in for a closer look. *He really is cute.* I sighed. *Devon. What kind of name is that?* I wondered. *Could be British. He looks sorta British. Maybe Devon has an accent—OMG . . . a British accent? JACKPOT!*

My face felt flushed, and I couldn't think straight. Devon had managed to climb into my mind. I looked around: there were photos of me and Mom all over the room. I didn't want her to see me like this. I took my note-book and scurried under the bed, where no one could see me, not even Mom's photos.

I started drawing and I couldn't stop. I drew all kinds of things—faces, mermaids, unicorns—and every picture included Devon. It was like my hand had a mind of its own.

"Mei-Mei?"

It was my mother. I bumped my head on the bed frame at the sound of her voice. I peered from underneath my bed. My heart froze. The door was opening. She couldn't find out what I was doing. I scrambled up onto the bed . . . and accidentally left the notebook on the floor. *Aaaahhh!*

Mom came in, carrying a plate of sliced fruit. "Mei-Mei, do you want a snack?"

"Cool! Great! Thanks!"

I was sweating buckets. The notebook peeked out from under my bed. *Don't look at the notebook, don't look at the notebook.* I smiled at her timidly. My mother seemed confused. I checked to see if the notebook was still on the floor . . . and my mother looked where I was looking. *No!*

She bent down to pick it up. And my future went up in smoke. "Is this your homework?" she asked, opening it.

I cringed. *Don't look through it, please don't look through it.*

But she did. Fully. "Oh, my—what—what is—*huh?*" She shrank back in disgust. "Mei-Mei, what is this?" She was horrified.

"It's nothing! Just a boy! He's no one!"

"A boy!" she shrieked. She held up a drawing of Devon and me kissing. "Who is this?" she demanded. "Did he do these things to you?"

I tried to grab the notebook from her. "*No!* It's just made up, Mom! It's not real!" But Mom wouldn't let go. I tried to convince her I made all of it up, but she wouldn't listen. She'd gone bonkers. *At least she won't recognize Devon from the drawing,* I thought. I could be thankful for that.

Suddenly, the notebook ripped apart. Mom looked at the drawing in her hands. "That hat . . . is that . . ." She had recognized him. *Curse my dynamic artistic abilities!* Mom shopped at Daisy Mart. She had memorized the face of every employee who worked there. "You never know who you'll have to identify in a police lineup," she once told me.

She charged from my room like a raging bull.

"Mom! No!"

10

The next thing I knew, we were in the car, with Mom in a rage at the wheel and me buckled into my seat like it was a straitjacket. "Mom, where are we going?" I pleaded. She wouldn't say. I was terrified. I had never screwed up like this before.

Mom drove like a wild person. She came within inches of running over two bike couriers and an elderly woman walking her dog. Finally, she swerved into a parking lot and told me to get out. She had my drawings in her hand. I saw where we were and gasped. *"What are you doing?"*

Mom had gone nuclear. We were at Daisy Mart.

Mom stormed into the store and made a beeline for the counter—where Devon was. "What've you done to my Mei-Mei?" She jabbed her finger at him like she was ready to stab him.

Devon fell back, totally confused. "Uh . . . who?"

I heard a snort behind us, followed by a familiar snarky laugh. "Meilin Lee, right here!"

I turned around and saw Tyler Nguyen-Baker laughing his head off. I wanted to crawl into a hole. Of all the people who had to see this, it was that weasel.

Mom fired accusations like darts at a dartboard. "I should report you to the police. How old are you? *Thirty?*" (For the record, Devon was clearly in high school.) "She's just a sweet, innocent child. How dare you take advantage of her!" Then she pulled out the big guns. She slammed my drawings onto the counter—for the whole world to see.

"Mom, *nooo!*"

The top drawing was the two-page spread of Devon as a merman. I felt like crying. The store was full of other kids from school, and they gathered around to take a better look. I turned away and closed my eyes. Everyone was laughing and snickering. My cheeks burned.

Mom looked Devon straight in the eye. "Daisy Mart has lost a loyal customer today!" she announced. Then she turned around and marched triumphantly out of the store. I heard Tyler cackling as we left.

Mom was practically doing a victory dance on the ride home. "Thank goodness I was here. That degenerate won't come near you again!"

I kept my mouth shut. I was too horrified to speak. *How can I face my friends after this? What are people at school going to say? Does she have any idea what she just did to me?*

Then, using the same tone my kindergarten teacher used to speak in, Mom asked, "Now is there anything else I should know about, Mei-Mei?"

"Aaaaaaaahhhhhh!"

I screamed into my pillow with all my might. I had acted like everything was all right on the way home, but it wasn't. After what had happened, how could it be?

"Aaaahhhhhhhhhhhh!"

The evening had been one bad thing after another. And it had started with those dumb drawings. "What were you *thinking?* Why would you draw those things? Those horrible, awful, sexy things!" I cried.

And then Mom had seen them and freaked out. Now she was in the living room, pretending nothing had happened, while Dad was in the kitchen, pretending nothing had happened. Meanwhile, I was on my bed, screaming my head off.

I couldn't show my face at school the next day, I realized. Kids from school had been there. And there was no way I could ever go to Daisy Mart again! Everyone there knew. And they'd tell others about me, too, and word would spread. Soon everyone would know about Mermaid Girl.

I got up and started pacing. *It's fine, you'll move to another city, change your identity. Sure, why not? I've always wanted to go to Buffalo.*

I stopped and looked at a photo of Mom and me. I must've been four or five, and there she was, smiling, so proud of her little Mei-Mei. My sweet, loving mother, *who* embarrassed the heck out of me in front of the entire world! Waves of anger surged inside me, and I felt my blood heating up.

"No, wait, I gotta calm down," I said to myself quickly. I turned away and started pacing again. "What am I thinking? I'm the one who started this. I'm the one who drew those things. My mother loves me. She wants only the best for me." I looked into the mirror. "You are her *pride* and *joy*, so act like it!"

I could barely stomach looking at myself. I felt so ashamed, so dirty. I was the one who had caused this. I had let my mom down. I had let my family down. *Why did I have to draw those things?* If I really was a Lee, I had to start acting like it.

I picked up my notebook and ripped the pages. Then I threw the whole thing in the garbage can. I went back to the mirror and looked myself straight in the eye. I made a solemn vow. "This will never happen again."

After all the drama of the evening, I was dead tired. I wanted to go to bed and forget that night ever existed.

The wind rattled the trees outside. It felt like there was going to be a big storm. I went to the window for a better look. The wind howled, and the branches of the courtyard trees heaved back and forth, ready to snap.

I climbed into bed and patted my stuffed dog on the head. "Things are going to be okay, right, Wilfred?" I asked. Then I turned off the lights and pulled the covers around me.

But I couldn't get any sleep—not real sleep. I kept tossing and turning all night, and I had strange dreams about the temple. I saw the stone pandas become menacing, their eyes glowing bright red. The statues cracked and then exploded, sending beams of white light toward the sky. Hundreds of pandas scurried over the temple roof like rats.

Then came bizarre, twisted images. I dreamed of Devon as the merman from my drawing, flopping around like a fish. Flowers bloomed, but they had the faces of 4*Town. A golden fan opened to reveal fractured images of my mother's face. She was screaming at me. Each scene jolted me like an electric shock.

Finally, I dreamed I was back at the temple, and the pandas around Sun Yee came alive. Their eyes burned red, and they leaped out of the tapestry, right at me. . . .

The next morning, I woke up feeling fuzzy. The sun knifed straight into my bedroom, and I didn't want to open my eyes. "I don't wanna get up," I moaned. My head felt groggy, like I'd hardly slept at all. The nightmares had been so intense and real.

Mom and Dad were in the kitchen, and the radio was on. From the amazing smells, I could tell Mom was making rice porridge.

"Mei-Mei, are you up?" she called out. "Breakfast is ready."

I smiled to myself. She had probably put a happy face made out of eggs and green onion on the porridge. It was the "Mei-Mei special."

As I lay in bed, I heard Mom's voice again. "*Ai-ya!* No sugar!"

Dad was trying to sneak in a pastry, just like he did every morning. And like every morning, Mom caught him.

I clomped out of bed, so tired, and waddled to the bathroom. Mentally, I began to put the day together. *I still have math to do,* I remembered. *Maybe I can finish it on the ride to school. Ack! Not that I want to go to school.* Memories of the train wreck at Daisy Mart hit me, and I groaned. I didn't know how I was going to face my friends after that. It was the worst thing that had ever happened to me.

I stepped into the bathroom and looked in the mirror. A giant red panda stared back. *This is strange. Did someone put up a panda poster?* I leaned in and looked again. The panda was kinda cute, actually. It had a huge head with big round eyes that looked just like mine. And when I smiled, the panda smiled, and when I pointed to the mirror, so did—

"Aaaaaahhhhhhhh!"

I fell back against the wall. My heart pounded, and I started hyperventilating. Slowly, I inched toward the mirror until my reflection came into view. "This isn't happening," I gasped. But there I was, a real red panda. I must've been eight feet tall. I reached up and touched my cheeks. Then I patted my stomach with my paws.

I *had paws?*

This is a dream, I thought. *I haven't woken up yet. This is part of my nightmare.* "Wake up, wake up, wake up," I muttered, and smacked myself. But nothing happened. This wasn't a dream. Tears fell down my giant furry face.

"Mei-Mei?" Mom knocked on the door. "Is everything okay?"

She couldn't see me like this. I swung around and—*thwomp!*—my tail knocked over everything around the sink.

Mom called out by the bathroom door. "Is it a fever? A stomachache? Chills? Constipation—"

"No!" I shouted. How could I explain this?

Then Mom gasped. "Wait. Is it . . . that? Did the red peony bloom?"

"No! Maybe?" *I dunno. What is she talking about?*

"Don't worry, Mei-Mei! I'll get you everything you need. Mommy's here!" Mom rushed away, shouting, "Jin, Jin, it's happening!"

I couldn't let either of them see me. I looked at the window and saw my chance to escape. I pulled myself up to the windowsill. "C'mon! Please!" I grunted, trying to push my giant head through. My tail thrashed behind me, sending bottles flying. But it was no use. I couldn't get out. And then my giant panda foot splashed into the toilet. *Ugh!*

"Mei-Mei, I'm coming!" Mom was going to come in.

"Crud! No!" I jumped into the bathtub and pulled the shower curtain around me. The door flew open, and Mom rushed into the room. "It's going to be okay!"

I hid behind the curtain. "No, it's not." I had just told her I didn't want her there. *"Will you just get out?"*

There was a pause. "Excuse me?" Mom replied in a prim voice.

Oh, no, I had just talked back to my mother.

"I didn't mean that!" Everything was going all wrong.

I wanted to cry. "I'm a gross red monster!" I wailed. *No! Mom can't know about this.* "Stop talking, stop talking . . ." I slapped my furry face.

"We're going to get through this together," Mom said. I could hear her rummaging through a box. "I have ibuprofen, vitamin B, a hot-water bottle . . ." Then she listed every type of pad known to humanity.

"Oh, no," I groaned. Mom thought I had gotten my period. I had to get her to leave. "Awesome!" I called out. "Just leave them by the sink."

She moved closer to the shower curtain. "Mei-Mei, perhaps we should talk about why this is happening," she began. "You are a woman now, and your body is starting to change."

Please don't say any more, please don't say any more, I willed her silently. This was horrifying. But she didn't stop. I stuffed my paws into my mouth to keep from screaming. This was worse than when my old gym teacher, Mrs. Clancy, taught health and hygiene and used pads as prizes for being student of the day.

"It's nothing to be embarrassed about," Mom continued.

"Mom! Please!"

As she spoke, I saw the shadow of her hand creep up behind the curtain: she was going to pull the shower curtain back!

"No! No, no, no, no!" I sputtered. The hand inched closer and grabbed hold of the curtain's edge. My knees buckled. "Oh, no . . ."

All of a sudden, a loud siren pierced the air, and Mom's hand stopped. The smoke alarm was going off. "My porridge!" she yelped, and rushed out.

A minute later, I peeked out the bathroom door. Clouds of smoke billowed in the kitchen, and Dad had broken out the fire extinguisher. I grabbed the chance to sneak out.

While my parents were rushing around, I tiptoed out to the hallway and into my bedroom. They didn't notice a thing. Then I closed the door behind me. I was finally alone.

I went straight to bed and pulled the covers over my

head. I didn't want to be awake a minute longer. "When I wake up, this will all be over."

The bed creaked from my gargantuan weight, and I heard a plank snap in two. I looked around for Wilfred, my best buddy. I had gotten him when I was in grade two. Wilfred always made me feel better. When I saw him, I breathed a sigh of relief.

Suddenly, there was a quiet *poof* by my ears. Pink clouds rose above me.

"What the . . ." I checked my head. The panda ears were gone.

I went to the mirror and saw my reflection. The ears really had disappeared. *Hey, this panda thing might not last forever,* I thought. I breathed easier and calmed down.

Once again . . . *poof!* I looked behind me. My tail had disappeared. "Whoa!"

My mind went into overdrive: *I think I might have figured out the on/off switch to this panda thing.*

Meanwhile, my face was itching like crazy. I wasn't used to having fur. I was about to use my paws to scratch.

Then I realized I had something better. I searched my room and found my hairbrushes. With one in each paw, I gently combed through the fur on my cheeks. "Mmm . . ." It felt sooo good, like a mini-spa on my face.

I closed my eyes and took a few deep breaths. This time, I heard a loud *poomph!* A cloud of pink covered me from head to toe. I looked down at my arms and legs and feet: I was human again. The panda had vanished. *I'm not a freak anymore.*

"*Yes!*" I shouted, and pumped my fist in the air.

Phwoom! Suddenly, I was back to panda mode. "*No!*"

So that's the key, I thought. *I think I know how to handle this.* I clasped my hands together and took deep breaths. I thought of calming images: the temple courtyard, birds in the sky, the CN Tower on a sunny day. And—*phwoom!*—I was back to being a girl.

I went to check myself in the mirror. I was back to being Meilin, the same as before, except for one thing: bright red panda–colored hair.

"Okay, no biggie," I said to myself. I could work with

that. *It's just hair,* I thought. *I know how to stay human. The rest is cake.*

I sat down on my bed and gave myself a quick pep talk. "You'll figure this out, Lee. Just be the calm, mature adult you totally are." It'd be like the panda thing had never happened. No one would ever know the difference.

To hide my new hair, I wore a sweet tuque to school. I figured no one would care, because everyone had bad hair days, right? Plus, tuques were very Canadian. I'd blend right in!

Mom insisted on driving me to school, and I tried to think calm thoughts in the car. *Be chill,* I said to myself.

As she pulled up to the curb, Mom turned to me. "I know it feels strange, Mei-Mei, but I promise, no one will notice a thing."

I wanted to gag. She still thought I had gotten my period. But I couldn't get upset—not now. *What person never, ever loses her cool?* I thought. *I have to be like her.*

"Thank you for your concern, Mother. But I'll be fine," I said, channeling the Queen, minus the accent.

Mom looked at me strangely. She gave me last-minute tips, then watched with worried eyes as I got out of the car. This was worse than my first day in kindergarten.

As I stepped through the front doors, I saw Miriam, Priya, and Abby right away. My heart skipped a beat. The 4*Townies were there! I wanted to hug them all but had to stop myself.

"Hey, girlfriends, what is up?" I said carefully as I strolled past. *Be chill, be chill,* I told myself.

They knew something wasn't right. Miriam asked about the tuque. Abby got a good whiff of me. (Why did red pandas have to smell so bad?) And Priya offered me her deodorant.

Then Miriam, looking completely serious, whispered in my ear, "Tyler's been telling everyone about the Daisy Mart."

Crud! I had completely forgotten about that. Abby went into full detail, and Priya said that he told everyone I was "kind of a perv."

Tyler was such a jerk! I wanted to wring his tiny little neck—*No! Be chill,* I reminded myself. *Be the Queen.* I calmed down right away and began to recite the events of the previous evening in a no-nonsense, factually correct manner.

Before I could finish, a head of thick, luxurious black hair passed by. Time seemed to slow down. It was Carter Murphy-Mayhew's hair. It was calling me. I wanted to reach out and touch it. . . .

Miriam's voice rang out. "Why are you staring at Carter Murphy-Mayhew?"

Ack! It was impossible to be chill here. Too many boys, too many feelings. The Queen had left the building.

Out of the corner of my eye, I saw a poster on the wall and froze. I recognized the drawing. *This can't be happening.* It was a photocopy of one of my sketchbook drawings of Devon. *Grrr!*

I ran to the wall and ripped it off. "No!" I cried out. Anger pulsed through my veins.

"Tyler keeps putting these up," Miriam said.

A loud snicker came from behind me, and I turned around. That obnoxious runt was across the hall, laughing at me.

"Knock it off, butthead!" Miriam yelled.

The other 4*Townies rushed to defend me.

"Not funny, Tyler!" Abby shouted. She, Miriam, and Priya made a wall in the hallway, shielding me from him.

"You're such a loser, Tyler!" called out Miriam.

My friends stood shoulder to shoulder, blocking him from my sight.

"I banish you. Begone," said Priya, who was probably quoting from her supernatural fantasy books.

But it didn't stop him. He kept on going. I could hear him trash-talking me, making loud kissing noises. I seethed. My hand tightened into a fist. I wanted to pound that weasel into the ground.

Then all of a sudden . . . *poof!* My fist became a panda paw. I scrambled to hide it, but there was another *poof* behind me. A fluffy tail shot out. "Oh, no . . ." I tried to stuff the tail into my skirt.

I had to get out of there. While the 4*Townies were dealing with Tyler, I backed away. "Gotta go! See you at lunch!" I shouted, and ran down the hall, trying to hide my panda-ness.

When I looked back to wave, I saw Miriam watching me, totally confused.

My nerves were about to explode. I had to calm down: I couldn't panda out. When I reached my classroom, I took a moment to find my zen and breathed deeply. The tail was gone. I was normal again. I chugged the herbal tea Mom had given me for good measure.

I was out of breath when I sat down. I rested my head on my desk and tried to get a hold of myself. Miriam sat next to me.

A girl who was a couple of seats away was eyeing me. "What's with her?" she asked Miriam.

"What's with your face?" Miriam answered.

Then Mir leaned toward me. "What *is* with you?" she whispered. "You're being weird."

I didn't know how I was going to make it through the day.

Mr. K was at the front of the class. He pointed to the chalkboard and announced, "The quadratic formula. Let the fun begin."

I remembered my unfinished math homework. But compared to everything else I had going on, that was no big deal. I could finish those math problems with one arm tied behind my back.

Miriam passed me a note asking if I was okay.

Yup! All good! I wrote back.

I meant it. For the next forty minutes, I could be the old Meilin. I owned that class. There wasn't anything in math I could not handle.

Miriam passed me another note, but I didn't bother reading it. I hoped she would get the hint that I wanted to pay attention. She pushed it closer to me and tapped it—this time insistent.

Finally, I took it and opened it up. Printed on the paper in her tidy handwriting were these four frightening words: *Your mom is outside.*

I looked out the window: Mom was wearing sunglasses and hiding behind a tree. I cringed and scooted down in my seat. "No, no, no, this isn't happening," I said under my breath.

"Uh, ma'am? Hi!" It was the security guard, Mr. Malik. I so badly wanted to be invisible. He didn't know what he was in for.

Suddenly, the voices got a lot louder. "I pay my taxes!" yelled my mom, and I heard Mr. Malik yelp in pain.

I couldn't bear to look. I should have known this might happen. On the first day of kindergarten, Mom got her head stuck in the schoolyard fence when she tried to get a peek at me during recess. It took three firefighters and a mechanical wire cutter to pry her away.

The other kids were clued in that something was going on. One by one, they got out of their seats to get a better view.

"All right, all right. Settle down, little goblins," said Mr. K. Then he went to the window himself to have a look. "Whoa."

All the kids ran to the window. My mom had turned into a bad reality TV show. One boy cried out, "Awesome! Full-on fight!"

I could hear them running around outside. Mom was probably leading Mr. Malik in circles. She had done Irish step dance as a teenager and could outmaneuver an opponent better than a professional basketball player.

"This is school property, ma'am," said Mr. Malik, breathless. "You are trespassing."

"Mei-Mei, tell him it's me!" my mother cried desperately. "Tell him it's Mommy!"

I kept my eyes on my desk. I was too horrified to look up. *I told Mom not to do this.* I fumed. *I told her I would be fine, but she treats me like I'm four years old.*

My jaw clenched, and I felt my temperature rising. *It's 'Mei-Mei this,' 'Mei-Mei that.' My real name is Meilin.* My hands tightened into fists. *She never listens to me! Now she* has embarrassed me in front of the whole school. I'm so mad I could—

"Tell him you forgot your pads!" Mom screamed.

Mr. K and the class fell back and collectively gasped. I knew what Mom was holding in her hands—for the whole world to see.

"Aaaaahhhh!" I roared.

Suddenly, there was a huge *pwoof!* Giant pink clouds exploded around me, sending desks and papers flying. I looked at myself: I had giant paws and red fur on my arms, legs, everywhere! *OMG, I just panda-ed out. . . .*

The whole classroom was thick with pink clouds. People were coughing. There was so much of it, no one could see. My heart raced, and I panicked. *I have to get out of here. I can't let anyone see me like this.*

Then I looked out the window and saw my mother staring straight at me. Our eyes locked. She was horrified. *She thinks her perfect daughter is an ogre now,* I thought.

I got out of there as fast as I could.

I lumbered into the hallway, crashing into garbage cans and carts with my giant panda body.

Hide! I said to myself. The only place I could think of was the girls' bathroom. I scrambled to get there. All my panda weight sloshed as I ran, and I ended up knocking over everything in my path. My heart pounded a thousand beats per minute.

"I can't believe this is happening," I whimpered.

I made it inside and moved the trash can to block the bathroom door. I was safe for the moment.

Right then, a girl came out of a stall. *No, not her!* It was Stacy Frick, one of the cool kids in my grade.

Stacy saw me in full panda mode, and her mouth dropped open. "O . . . M—"

I quickly put my paw over her face and shoved her back into the stall. Meanwhile, people were banging on the door to get in. I couldn't stay.

The only exit was the window. I jumped up, pushed my body through, and landed on the school grounds outside. I scanned for people left and right. It felt like I was being hunted. I took a deep breath and tried to calm down. *I have to get home,* I thought. *That's the only place that's safe.*

I wanted to run home without being seen, but it was no use. No matter where I went, I caused trouble. I wasn't used to claws and a tail and a hulking eight-foot body. I dodged into an alleyway.

When I exited on the other side, I crashed into a couple walking by. "It's a monster!" the man cried, and they both fled in terror.

I caught sight of another narrow alley between two buildings. *No one will see me there.* I dove in, but my stupid giant body didn't fit. I had to squeeze my way through, and I dragged my fur along the sides of the buildings. When I made it to the other side, I was coated in garbage and slime.

I kept running. *I have to get home, I have to get home,*

I thought, panting. But then I turned and glanced into a store window. It was Daisy Mart. *OMG, is that Devon?* My brain instantly melted at the sight of him.

"*Aaoogahh!*" I blurted out.

Devon turned around. *Oh, no, he can't see me like this!* And I fled.

My mind was racing. Everything seemed to be a blur. Everywhere I turned, cars were honking at me, and one car screeched to a stop to avoid hitting me. I looked up and saw the rooftops and had an idea. *That's how I'll get home!*

Slowly, I climbed a fire escape ladder, hauling up my bulky panda frame. (Why couldn't I be as small as an actual red panda? *Aaarrgghh!*) I scrambled and nearly fell a few times but finally made it to the top. *Gotta get home, gotta hide!*

The city skyline lay before me, with all the rooftops lined up and ready. I was out of breath, panting, but I knew how to get home.

I hurled myself across rooftops. I stumbled from one

building to the next but kept moving forward. At last, the temple came into view, and I felt like crying. *I see home!*

I made one final giant leap toward the temple, sailed through the air . . . and belly flopped against the court-yard wall. I collapsed onto the sidewalk and broke down crying. *No, no, no! I almost made it!* I got up and rushed through the gates.

By the time I got into the house, I was sobbing buckets. I couldn't think straight. I saw all the familiar things: my living room, my family photos, my bedroom. But they didn't belong to me. *This isn't my home,* I thought, crying. *It belongs to a girl named Meilin Lee.* I staggered around, looking at all the reminders of the little girl who had lived there. My tail thrashed, smashing into furniture.

I went to my bedroom, my safe space. *Where's Wilfred? He always makes things better.* There he was, on my bed, just like that morning, and I sighed in relief. I grabbed my hairbrushes and hid under a blanket. I furiously brushed my face again and again. When I did that before, it had made me turn human.

"Mei-Mei?" someone called out from the door. It was my mom.

I burst into tears again. "Don't look at me!" I sniffed. "Stay back!" I couldn't let her see me. She would run away from me, too.

Mom came in. "Sweetie, it's okay. Mommy's here," she said gently. She didn't seem surprised at all. She knelt down by my side as I continued to sob.

"What's happening to me?" I wailed.

Right then, my dad rushed into the room. "What is it?" Then he looked at me and Mom. "It's happened already?"

Already? "What did you say?"

Gently, Dad placed a hand on Mom's shoulder. "Ming, it's time."

Silently, my parents walked me to the main hall of the temple. Tears fell down my face as we went through the courtyard, past the trees and the koi fish pond. I was still in panda mode.

Nothing's the same anymore, I thought, crying. *I don't belong here.*

My parents were solemn, their faces showing lines of worry.

When we entered the hall, Mom went to the portrait of Sun Yee. Instead of bowing, like she normally did, she lifted the tapestry. Behind it was a secret compartment in the wall.

Whoa, where did that come from? I'd never seen it before.

Mom reached in and took out a box. She gave a heavy sigh as she placed it on the altar. "As you know, our ancestor Sun Yee had a mystical connection with red pandas." Inside the box was a scroll with frayed edges. Mom continued, "In fact, she loved them so much that she asked the gods to turn her into one."

The scroll showed images of Sun Yee turning into a panda.

What was going on? "Why did she . . . How could . . ." I sputtered.

As Mom unrolled the scroll, she began the story. "It was wartime. The men were all gone. Sun Yee was desperate for a way to protect herself and her daughters. Then, one night, during a red moon, the gods granted her wish. They gave her the ability to harness her emotions to transform into a powerful mystical beast."

I couldn't believe what I was hearing.

"She was able to fend off the bandits, protect her village, and save her family from ruin. Sun Yee passed this gift to her daughters for when they came of age. And they passed it to theirs. But over time, our family chose to come to a new world. And what was a blessing became . . . an inconvenience."

I looked up at Sun Yee, this figure I had revered my entire life. I said slowly, "Are . . . you . . . *serious?*"

I wanted to scratch her to bits.

My parents gasped. "Mei-Mei, no!" shouted my mother as they tried to hold me back.

"It's a curse!" I shouted at Sun Yee. "It's a *curse!* You cursed us! It's all your fault!"

"She meant it as a blessing!" Mom cried.

I charged at Sun Yee again, and my parents tried to grab hold of me. The altar shook, and objects went flying. *Who cares about this ancient nonsense, anyhow? It's not like Sun Yee cared about us.*

My parents finally managed to force me back from the altar. They were both out of breath, shaken.

"Why didn't you warn me?"

Mom sighed. "I thought I had more time! You're just a child! I thought if I watched you like a hawk and never left your side, I'd see the signs, be able to prepare!"

She paused and collected herself for a moment. "But it's going to be fine. I overcame it, and you will, too."

My mother lifted the jade pendant around her neck and held it out to me. "On the next red moon, you'll undergo a ritual that will seal your red panda spirit into one of these." The pendant gleamed in front of me. "And then you'll be cured for good, just like me."

I had thought Mom's necklace was some sort of lucky charm. But all that time, the jade was hiding a fierce spirit inside.

She explained that any strong emotion would release the panda, and the more it was released, the more challenging the ritual would become. "There is a darkness to the panda, Mei-Mei," Mom cautioned me. Her face became grim. "You only have one chance to banish it, and you cannot fail. Otherwise, you'll never be free."

The warning gave me chills.

Meanwhile, Dad was checking a calendar nearby. "Let's see . . . the next red moon will be on the twenty-fifth," he said calmly, as though he were planning one of his barbecues.

"That's a whole month away!" I cried.

Mom took my paws in her human hands. "We'll wait it out together. And I'll be with you every step of the way."

I managed to calm down enough to poof back into a girl, but it was a constant struggle. Later that night, Dad and I dragged the mattress back into my room, and Mom brought in bedding. My folks had stripped my room bare that evening, taking out my desk, my shelves, and my posters. All I had left was a mattress and Wilfred. I held him close to me.

"It's only temporary, Mei-Mei," Mom said as she tucked me in. "This way we won't worry about any more . . . accidents."

That was how Mom described the way I had wrecked the house that day. The whole living room was destroyed and covered with fur. Plus, I had broken my own bed that morning. All because I had lost control.

Once I was settled, Mom and Dad wished me good night. Dad lingered by the door after Mom left. He looked uncomfortable. He hadn't said much since he found out about my panda, but that was typical. He didn't say much normally. But sometimes, unexpectedly, he would say just the right thing.

Dad paused. Then, just as he was about to close the door, he said brightly, "Red is a lucky color."

I guessed that wasn't one of those times.

My parents began speaking in hushed tones in the kitchen. "This is awful. What are we going to do?" asked my mom. Dad tried to comfort her, but Mom sounded terrified. "No one can see her like this. Did you see how she was in the temple? Her eyes . . ."

I started crying.

"I can't even look at her like this," Mom continued.

My heart broke in two. Suddenly, I heard a *phwoom:* I had poofed into a panda again. I curled into a ball, tucking my tail under me, and tried to shut out their voices. I hugged Wilfred even tighter.

After explaining the red panda curse to me, Mom had

assured me that she still loved me. As I lay there, I heard loud and clear that it wasn't me she loved. It was a girl named Mei-Mei.

The next morning, Mom put up a sign on the temple gates: CLOSED! DUE TO FAMILY EMERGENCY. All the tours and meetings were canceled. It was the first time the temple had ever shut down like that.

Mom told me that afterward, the tai chi seniors got really grumpy about being turned away, and some threatened to picket if the temple didn't open again. Mr. Gao had shown up for our weekly chess match, but Mom told him I couldn't make it. She said he was disappointed but he understood. Then he made an odd comment to her: that "it was bound to happen."

My folks stayed at home and did a massive cleanup of the living room and hallway. They were frightened one of the neighbors might see me ("We can't have them calling the police"), so they closed all the drapes and bolted all the doors to the house. Meanwhile, I stayed in my bedroom and had to act like I didn't exist.

My parents told me again and again they loved me and said everything was going to be okay. But it was hard to believe. I wasn't allowed to leave my room and have breakfast with them. My folks put food on a plate and slid it into my room "just to be safe." And when they spoke to me, they never looked me in the face. My own parents couldn't bear to look at me.

I huddled alone in my room with Wilfred. "I'm a freak, I'm a monster," I cried, sobbing into my mattress. "I wish this had never happened. I wish *I* had never happened."

I couldn't control my panda. Sometimes I would be human. But then I would hear Mom getting upset or I'd worry about never seeing my friends again, and—*poof!*—I would panda out.

I just wanted to be normal again. *"Aaaaggh!"* I grunted as I slammed my panda self into the walls. *"Ergghh!"* I wanted to stamp out those panda parts.

"Please . . . just . . . go . . . away," I cried. But no matter how hard I tried, they would poof right back.

I looked at my best buddy—my only buddy. *Wilfred, will it always be like this?*

Suddenly, I heard tapping noises on the window. I looked over. *What's going on?* I wondered.

"Mei, it's us! Open up!" It was Miriam. My friends were there.

"Crud, no!" I cried. I was in full panda mode. I jumped up and clutched the curtains, trying to stay hidden. *They can't see me like this.*

"Are you okay? Tap if you can hear us!" called out Priya.

"One for yes, two for no!" added Abby.

I loved the 4*Townies, and they meant everything in the world to me. I would have done anything to see them, *but not then*!

"We thought you died of embarrassment!" said Miriam.

I tried to think of what to do. Maybe my mom could shoo them away.

But then Abby shouted something that made my heart leap a mile high. "4*Town's coming to Toronto!"

"What?"

I ripped open the curtains and looked straight into the faces of my very human friends. Their eyes bugged out, and their jaws dropped. Then all of them started screaming.

"Hey, shhh!" I quickly pulled my friends through the window and into my room. I muffled their mouths against my fur. I had to get them to stop freaking out. "It's okay! It's me. It's Mei. Calm down, all right?"

Their eyes were as big as table tennis balls. I explained carefully, "I'm gonna let go, and you're gonna be chill, got that?"

All three looked up at me and slowly nodded. I gently let them go, and they all stared at me with their mouths open. *Please don't be scared,* I thought. *I'm still Mei. I'm still your friend.*

They couldn't believe it was me. They didn't say anything for a long time.

"Mei?" Miriam finally asked, like she was checking to see that I was real.

"Are you a werewolf?" Priya blurted out.

Uh, excuse me?

"She's a red panda!" Abby squealed. She ran up, delighted, and buried her face in my belly. Out of all of us, Abby loved animals the most. "You're so fluffy!" She nuzzled my fur with her whole face. *"You're so fluffy!"*

The other girls followed, checking me out. Priya inspected my tail. "I've always wanted a tail," she said admiringly.

Uh, I'm not a character in one of your supernatural novels, Priya.

Finally, Miriam asked me what had happened.

I took a deep breath and tried to explain in the least terrifying way possible. "It's just some, you know, inconvenient, uh . . . genetic thingy I got from my mom." Tears welled up in my eyes. My friends might never see the normal me again. "It'll go away eventually, maybe . . ." I broke down crying.

My friends rushed to comfort me.

"I hate this," I said, choking down sobs. "I'm slobby, I'm smelly . . . my mom won't even look at me."

What good am I to anyone as a panda? And now 4*Town is coming to Toronto. It was my lifelong dream to see them. Wiping away tears, I asked when the concert was.

"May eighteenth! They just announced it!" Abby answered.

My heart sank. I told them about the red moon ritual that would take place on May twenty-fifth. "There's no way this'll be gone by then! Just go . . . go become women without me." My life was over.

"Mei, it's going to be okay," said Miriam.

She was trying to be nice, but it was no use. She didn't know what would happen. *I might be like this forever.* The thought made me tear up again.

"Just . . . just leave me alone," I said. I took Wilfred in my arms and curled up on the floor. It was the two of us from now on.

I tried to shut out the world, but the familiar sounds of

beatboxing started up above me. Two other voices chimed in. I couldn't believe it: my friends were doing "Nobody Like You." It was the anthem song for the 4*Townies.

I knew they wanted me to join in, but I couldn't. I wasn't one of them. Then Miriam began singing the lyrics, and soon all of them were singing. I looked up. My friends were dancing. They were using their hands as microphones. *OMG, they're doing the moves to the whole routine.*

The girls paused, and Miriam held out her hand mic, wanting me to join in. I hesitated, but they waited. Quietly, I sang the next line. I wasn't sure what they'd do, but my friends all joined in with the chorus, just like before.

My heart opened up. We were still the 4*Townies! I wanted to hug every one of them. I got up and joined in, for real this time, and the four of us danced and sang and laughed until the end of the song.

"Thanks, guys. You're the best," I said. They really were.

My friends gathered around me, and I felt at home again. "You're our girl," Priya said.

"Yeah, no matter what," added Miriam. "Panda or no panda."

The 4*Townies all hugged, and I felt huge waves of gratitude come over me. Then, suddenly—*phwoom!*—a pink cloud appeared.

Miriam gasped, and Abby was stunned.

"Whoa, Mei!" exclaimed Priya, slack-jawed.

I was human again, with one red difference.

Miriam loved the new hair.

"Red looks *so* good on you," said Priya.

Abby trudged toward me, barging past Miriam, and eyed me up and down. "Is it gone?"

I started to explain that I would turn into a panda again if I got overly excited. Then Abby pinched my cheek. "Ow! Abby, what the heck?" *You can't just do that to someone. You need permission.*

Wait . . . I'm mad, but I'm still human.

"Huh," I said to myself, baffled. "Something feels . . . different."

A germ of an idea percolated in my brain. *Hey, maybe*

this can work. I had a theory I wanted to test. I tapped my arm and said, "Abby, hit me." Abby had a green belt in aikido, and I knew she could control—

She punched me in the face.

Down I went, sprawling on the floor. But a minute later, woozy but human, I managed to get up on my feet. There was no sign of the panda anywhere.

"Oh my gosh, I stayed calm! Something about you guys, like, neutralizes the panda!"

"Aw! It's our love!" exclaimed Miriam.

"We're like a warm and fuzzy blanket," added Priya.

I backtracked and began to piece together what this meant for me: it meant everything. "I can have my room back . . . I can have my life back."

"Even better . . . you can come with us to 4*Town!" Miriam's voice broke through my thoughts.

"Huh?" What was she talking about?

It turned out my friends had decided they were going to ask their parents that night if they could go to the concert.

"We're making our stand," said Priya.

Abby was totally hyped up. "You in or you out?"

What were they thinking? There was no way Mom would let me go. "I'm a furry ticking time bomb," I said.

"A time bomb of awesomeness!" Miriam argued. "And now you can control it."

"I dunno, my mom's worried that—"

"Mei, you're not just someone's daughter," Miriam interrupted. "You're one of us!"

"Yeah, you're a 4*Townie!" cried Abby.

"And 4*Townies are fierce. We don't back down from a challenge," said Priya.

"Or wolves," joked Miriam.

"Or bears!" exclaimed Abby. Then she looked at me. "No offense."

"Technically, red pandas aren't bears," Priya said. Of course she'd be logical about this.

Suddenly, I heard a voice in the hallway. "Mei-Mei?"

It was my mother. I panicked. I had to get my friends

out of my room. Mom would go ballistic if she knew they were there.

Mir wanted to talk more, but I hustled her out the window. "My mom already doesn't like you," I said, accidentally letting it slip.

Miriam looked confused. "Wait, she doesn't?"

Once my friends were gone, I slammed the window shut and closed the drapes tight. Mom opened the door just as I turned, breathless. A little nervous, she looked around my room. "Is everything okay? I thought I heard—"

I stopped her short. I had made a decision. "Mom, I think I've made a breakthrough."

When I told my mom about my new ability, she looked hesitant. "I'm not entirely sure, Mei-Mei," she said.

"But it works!"

I had done it with my friends. I could do it again. All it took was a bit of Mei Power!

"I swear I can control this. You don't have to be afraid anymore."

She sighed. "I'll discuss this with your father. If you think this might work . . ."

"Better than that: I *know* it will."

My parents murmured in the hallway. "We have to be absolutely certain," I heard Mom say.

Shortly after, she came back to my room. "Your father and I have come to an agreement. We're going to set a test for you. If you're able to control your feelings, things can go back to normal until the ritual."

I jumped for joy. *"Thank you! That's awe—"* I caught myself and calmed down. "I mean . . . thank you for your flexibility. Please thank Father for me."

She still seemed wary. "But you have to pass the test."

I almost laughed. *A test? Meilin Lee has never failed a test.*

While my parents were getting ready, I practiced in my room. I pictured things that made me mad enough to scream: Tyler Nguyen-Baker, that night at Daisy Mart. But every time I saw those things in my head, I pictured the 4*Townies coming to my rescue.

"Who's going to remember stuff like that in ten years?" I heard Miriam saying. "We'll be the biggest pop stars in the world by then!"

Finally, Mom came into my room and told me they were ready.

I sat at the kitchen table, armed and prepared. But my parents came ready, too. They gave each other pointed looks, then started the test. In my dad's hands were photos that were bound to push my buttons. One by one, he showed them to me.

"Deforestation," Mom announced. The photo showed land devastated by man's never-ending greed. But I didn't lose my cool.

"Sad orangutan." It was an orangutan trapped in a metal cage. I squirmed. *Animals shouldn't live in cages.* Ever since I was eight, I had refused to eat eggs that weren't from free-range hens. But I stayed calm.

Then Dad showed a photo of a younger me looking disappointed. It was my second-place finish at the spelling bee.

I almost lost it. I should have won that tournament! I only came in second place because I had studied from an American dictionary and the judges only considered the Canadian spelling for the final word.

But suddenly, I heard the voices of the 4*Townies. I pictured them around me, comforting me.

"The most important thing is you tried," said Miriam.

"You spelled your little butt off," noted Priya.

Finally, Abby told me that I was first place in their hearts. It was so peaceful I calmed down right away. Who cared about a first-place trophy?

I took a deep breath. "What . . . a . . . shame," I said calmly to my parents.

They looked impressed. I breathed a sigh of relief. I didn't panda out. I was going to ace the test.

Then Mom looked at Dad, and he got up from the table. He returned with a box and set it down in front of me. Both my parents backed away. I heard a faint noise coming from the box, then another. *No, it can't be! This isn't fair!*

Slowly, I opened the box. *Kittens!* It was a whole box of tiny cute kittens. One of the stray cats that hung around the temple had just given birth to a litter. These must've been them.

"So . . . cute," I muttered. They were adorable. I tensed up and grabbed hold of my pants to keep myself from petting them. The kittens started crawling over me. I broke into a sweat. "Must . . . resist," I grunted.

I loved cats. I drew them all the time. I had pleaded for one, but Mom had said no. She told me that she didn't want an animal in the house, because the house would get dirty. *Wait a minute—she was worried about one tiny kitten. Meanwhile, she knew the entire time I would become a panda!*

An image zoomed into my brain. I was surrounded by adorable kittens cuddling me. But then in my mind, the kittens morphed into human girls, the 4*Townies. Now I was surrounded by my friends. I calmed down. I was safe.

"We love you, girl," they told me.

"Panda or no panda," Miriam added.

Then I opened my eyes—my human eyes—and said to my parents, rationally, "How adorable."

My parents gasped. They couldn't believe it.

"*How is this possible? What happened to your panda?*" asked Mom.

I started to explain. "When I get emotional, all I do is picture the people I love most in the whole world . . ."

Mom got a tender look on her face. She leaned toward me, toward her Mei-Mei. *Oh, boy . . .*

". . . which is you guys."

I didn't have the nerve to tell her the truth. I would someday, when I was away at university, studying abroad with an ocean and two continents separating us.

Mom came in to hug me. "Oh, Mei-Mei," she cooed.

I hugged her back. Then I realized that was the perfect time to ask her a really big question. "I just have one teeny tiny favor to ask."

I asked Mom if she and Dad could spare a few minutes later that day. I had an important matter to discuss. She said yes right away (I'm her favorite daughter, after all!), and I got to work.

I figured my parents weren't going to agree to a concert if I just came out and asked. This was a big deal. It required finesse.

Meanwhile, my folks moved some of my stuff back into my room. I put Wilfred on my shelf for inspiration, sat down at my desk, and prepared my plan of attack.

I decided to do a presentation that would argue in favor of my attending the upcoming 4*Town concert. In a series of slides with clip art and graphics, I would outline the multiple benefits and positive consequences of going to the concert of the century in the company of my extremely mature and trustworthy friends.

If anyone could pull this off, it was me. Who was the Toronto District School Board junior debating champ? Me. Who reduced the Ontario Science Fair judges to tears with her multisensory exhibit about the dying coral of the Great Barrier Reef? No one but me. I even had the foresight to bring an extra box of tissues to the final round of judging. *This will totally work!* I thought as I planned out everything.

I searched the back room cupboards of the house for props to enhance the presentation. Then I quickly practiced my cartwheels for a memorable ending. Every little bit helped. With all this Mei Power, how could they say no?

"No, absolutely not!" Mom practically shouted at me.

I was kneeling in front of my final slide, which compared 4*Town to the great classical composers. I had a hard time breathing. It had been a long time since I'd done a backflip. My sparklers were lit up in my hands. I was wearing my lucky green blazer. And she still said no.

"But this is once in a lifetime," I whined.

Mom said it was one thing for home or school. But a concert? "You'll get whipped up into a frenzy and panda all over the place."

My father had been studying the 4*Town pamphlet I had created. "Ming, maybe we should trust her," he said quietly.

Mom pointed to my 4*Town slide, her finger stabbing the air like a knife. "It's *them* I don't trust. Look at those glittery delinquents with their . . . gyrations."

Why couldn't she understand that 4*Town was the best?

Mom turned to me and asked why I wanted to go so badly.

Images immediately zoomed into my mind: Me, Miriam, Priya, and Abby dancing onstage at the concert, tens of thousands of fans cheering us on. There would be lights and frenzy and music, culminating with each 4*Townie being lifted into the air by her favorite member of 4*Town.

I snapped back to reality. "I just want to broaden my musical horizons," I answered.

My mom didn't buy it. She said no. She said that my dad said no. "No concert. And that's final."

Well, that was that. I politely thanked them for listening and took down my presentation. But I wasn't happy about it. My parents watched me go to my room. I threw a look back at Mom. *Humph. Who needs you, anyhow?* Then I slammed my door.

"*What was that?*" I heard Mom say behind my door. She could get angry, too, for all I cared. All I wanted was this one little thing, and she said no.

I got out my CD player and put on my headphones. The phone rang, and I heard Dad telling my mom that Grandma was on the line. My grandmother lived in Florida, and I hardly ever saw her. I pressed play and drowned them out.

Who wants to be part of this dumb family, anyway? I bet Mom had never felt this way. She'd never understand.

"Where are we going?" I asked Dad.

"You'll see," he said.

After dinner, Dad had suggested to Mom that he take me out for a drive. That way I could get used to being in public again before school the next day.

Dad made a left turn and pulled up to a plaza. He stopped the car right in front of the donut shop.

"No way! You're taking me here?" I asked.

He unbuckled his seat belt and winked at me. "Don't tell Mom."

Dad ordered a coffee and a honey cruller, and I got a chocolate donut with sprinkles. We took our tray and sat by the window. I was starving, actually. I hadn't eaten during dinner. I hadn't said much to my parents, either. I was too mad.

Dad took a few sips of his coffee and rubbed his temples. We sat across from each other. He looked tired.

Finally, he spoke. "I wanted to check in with you, kiddo, see how you're doing."

I pretended that I couldn't talk because my mouth was full.

"I know it's been rough these past few days. I'm sorry about that." He grabbed hold of his mug and took another sip. He spoke slowly, being careful. "I wanted to tell you that it's not been easy for your mom and me to handle, either. This is new for us, too."

You could let me go to the concert, I thought.

Dad took a bite of his cruller, and a big smile spread across his face. "It's been a long time since I've had one of these. Your mom's careful with my diet."

I stared at my plate. "If you live at our house, you have to do everything she says," I groused.

Dad chuckled and finished his bite. "Your mom means well, sweetheart," he said lightly. "She was your age once too, y'know."

If she knew how I felt, she would understand how

important the concert was. "Why doesn't she let me go? Why doesn't she trust me?"

Dad sighed and leaned back in his chair. He looked around the donut shop. It was pretty empty, with only a few customers and the cashier.

He turned to me again and changed the topic. "Your grandmother called tonight."

"How's she doing?" Grandma was my mother's mother. Mom didn't talk about her much. I never got the feeling they were close the way Mom and I were.

"She was concerned about you," he said.

"Oh." *Grandma probably wouldn't let me go see 4*Town, either,* I thought gloomily.

Dad didn't say anything more about the call. Instead, he checked his watch. "It's about time we head back. We don't want to worry your mother."

I finished eating and got up. Dad helped me into my jacket. When he was done, he put his hand on my shoulder. "Your mom and I will always love you, Mei. We may not be able to show it the way you want us to, but we do. Remember that."

I knew he meant it. "Thanks, Dad," I said, and kissed him on the cheek.

He looked at the front counter and laughed. "How about we sneak a few donuts for the ride home, eh?"

I smiled back. Sometimes he did say just the right thing.

The news had spread that 4*Town was coming to Toronto. The next morning, everyone was talking about it at school. It seemed like half the kids were going to the concert. Lucky them. The only upside was that no one noticed that I'd been away or that I had come back with different hair.

Miriam, Priya, Abby, and I had all struck out with our parents. None of them would let us go. They didn't approve of the music (Abby's parents), thought we were too young (Priya's), or wouldn't shell out the money for tickets (Miriam's).

The 4*Townies complained about it during phys ed. Mr. K took the class outside to play dodgeball.

Abby replayed a huge fight she'd had the night before with her folks. "Mine called it stripper music! What's wrong with that?" she fumed, ducking an oncoming ball.

The only one who came close to a yes was Miriam, but she would have to pay for the ticket herself. "Who the heck's got that kind of cash?" Miriam complained.

As for my own parents, well, midway through the game, Miriam told me to look across the street. Parked in a familiar car was a familiar head of glossy hair. She had been there the whole morning.

Mr. Malik approached the car, waving his arms. "Ma'am, please! Sorry, Mrs. Lee, I see you!"

Mom shouted something at him. (I wasn't sure what, but probably cursing.) Then she took one last look at me and drove off.

Sheesh. How did I end up with a parent like this?

I turned around and caught Tyler snickering at me. He wasn't the only one. "Little mama's girl," he said, cackling.

"That guy is such a jerk," I muttered. I was holding a ball in my hands, and I gripped it tight. *I want to hurl this thing right at his big mouth.*

"No wonder Mei's such a loser!" He got other kids to join in. Soon they were all laughing.

Grrr! I wanted to pound him into the ground. Waves of rage surged inside me. *Poof!* My arm turned into a giant panda arm. I eyed Tyler's fat head and whipped that ball with all my panda strength.

"*Aaah!*" Tyler cried. He ducked as the ball barely missed his head. It zoomed past him, rocketing through the air, and smashed a school window.

Mr. K blew his whistle. "Illegal throw! You're out, Lee!"

Hey, I'm the one who gets thrown out? "But, Mr. K, he—" I started to protest.

The 4*Townies took hold of me and hustled me off the court. The whole class was watching me.

"You need to chill," Miriam whispered into my ear.

My friends took me straight to the girls' bathroom. I was ready to lose it. *That stupid Tyler! I should've gone full panda right there.* I fumed. *That would've made him stop laughing.* My friends were worried.

"Calm down, Mei," Miriam told me.

"Dude, keep it together," said Priya.

I didn't want to be calm. There was too much to be

upset about. First off, I was going to miss the chance of a lifetime to see 4*Town. "We *need* to see this concert. Why doesn't my mom get that?" I had spent my entire life being calm, doing all the things my mom wanted me to. I paced back and forth, listing them. "Temple duties, grades . . ."

"Violin!" added Abby.

"Tap dancing!" chimed in Priya.

Yeah, my friends knew what I was talking about. They knew the score.

"We've been *so* good. If they don't trust us anyway, then what's the point?" I argued.

Miriam looked at me and smiled. She was impressed. "Wow, who *are* you? I love it!"

Who was I? Not Mei-Mei—at least, not anymore. Right there and then, I realized that that part of my life was over. Seeing 4*Town would seal it for good.

I held out my hands to the 4*Townies. "This isn't just our first concert," I said to them solemnly. "This is our first step into womanhood. And we have to do it together."

My friends put their hands on mine, all of us making an unspoken vow. Destiny was calling.

"I'm in, girl!" Miriam said, backing me up. "We'll say it's a sleepover at my house."

Abby called it the perfect crime.

I had to admit it was perfect. Mom would never know the difference.

Next we needed money, and 4*Town tickets weren't cheap. We had to figure out a way to raise enough cash in just a few weeks.

"Come on, let's think," I said.

Abby had a gleam in her eye. "Know what'll help me think? A little panda." I didn't want to break it out, but she insisted. "It'll clear my mind . . . it's so cute!"

I gave in. As Abby snuggled against me, I imagined Robaire as a merman—a *French*-speaking merman. My heart leaped with joy. Then I heard a familiar *phwoom*, and Abby was suddenly nuzzling the fur of a red panda.

Right then, the bathroom door flew open, and I heard

a sharp gasp. Stacy Frick and her friends were standing there in their gym clothes. They were staring at me with their mouths wide open.

"OMG ..." Stacy cried.

I panicked and raced into a stall. *It's game over.* I groaned. My friends stood outside the door, blocking me from Stacy and her crew.

Stacy wouldn't budge. "That was *you* in the bathroom! I didn't imagine it!"

She and her friends tried to figure out what kind of creature I was. One guessed "magical bear." I rolled my eyes. *Magical bear, gimme a break.*

"Red panda!" my friends and I corrected them.

Then the strangest thing happened: Stacy and her friends went totally fangirl. "You are the cutest thing ever!" cried Stacy. They all begged me to come out.

"Wait, so you like the panda?" I said, slowly coming out of hiding.

"Like it? I *love* it!" one girl squealed.

I don't have to hide who I am, I realized. I looked at my friends, amazed.

Stacy and her friends mobbed me. They couldn't get enough panda. They said they would give anything for more panda—their soul, their internal organs. Even money.

Uh . . . money?

I looked at Miriam, Priya, and Abby, and we all smiled. We had just found the solution we were looking for.

When Stacy and her friends finally left, my friends and I brainstormed about how to raise the money.

A light bulb went on in my head. "We'll do it like the fanfic!" I said. It was the perfect plan. "We already have a ton of ideas for the 4*Townies: merchandising, marketing, videos. We'll do the same for the panda."

My friends loved it.

"We can ask my cousin for help," said Miriam, getting excited. "He works at a souvenir shop. They make their own T-shirts."

Priya and Abby both did a fist pump.

"We'll raise that money in no time!" Abby cried.

Tickets were two hundred dollars apiece, so the goal was to raise eight hundred dollars in only a few weeks. We had to hustle, but we could do it.

First we had to figure out how to run this operation

without raising eyebrows. We would use the school as our base, but the teachers couldn't find out about it.

Next there was a certain someone we had to get out of our hair: the Notorious M.I.N.G. I knew the perfect way to do it.

When class ended that afternoon, my friends gathered around the school pay phone while I made an important call.

"Mathletes?" Mom said, surprised. "Isn't it a little dangerous to join an after-school club now?"

I had come prepared. "What's dangerous is an academic record with a lack of extracurriculars." I knew Mom would agree with that. And she did.

The 4*Townies commandeered an unused classroom for our headquarters. We filled the room with math textbooks and posters as camouflage. We were ready for business.

I was kinda nervous about showing the panda to everyone. I didn't know what to expect—what if they actually didn't like me? During class, the 4*Townies passed around notes announcing the first Red Panda Girl photo op. When we went to set up at lunch hour, kids were already lining up down the hall. It was wild! They couldn't wait to meet and take photos with me. R.P.G. was a rock star!

During that time, I had gotten pretty good at poofing into and out of the panda. I didn't really have to think about it. As long as I kept my cool, it felt as natural as breathing.

For the next stage of our plan, Miriam contacted her cousin, and we had panda T-shirts made up. The girls and I created a line of fun merchandise to sell, like panda ears and tails.

The cash poured in. Within a day or two, we had already reached two hundred dollars.

Miriam, Priya, and I celebrated at HQ. "4*Town forevah!" we shouted.

Mom didn't suspect a thing. "How was Mathletes, Mei-Mei?" she called out when I got home late. She had the dumpling ingredients placed in front of her. "Come quickly. *Jade Palace Diaries* has already started."

Dozens of kids had lined up for photos after school, and now I had to finish making more panda ears for the next day.

"Uh, thanks, but I've got homework," I said, hustling to my room.

A few minutes later, there was a soft knock. I opened the door to see Mom standing in the hallway, holding a plate. "I brought you some dumplings, Mei-Mei. I thought you could use a snack."

"This is great. Thanks, Mom!" I took the plate and began to close the door.

"Mr. Gao was at the temple today," she said. "He asked about you."

Crud, our chess game! "Tell him I'll be there for a rematch soon, I promise!"

I glanced behind me. The panda merchandise and money were all stored under my bed. I couldn't let her in. "I can't talk now," I said nervously. "Lots of studying."

Mom looked a bit sad when I closed the door, but I couldn't think about that. I had to get working again.

As part of the 4*Townie journey, I borrowed Dad's camcorder. According to Priya, the most important bands kept a behind-the-scenes video diary of their major tours. She argued that in twenty years, the 4*Townies would want a souvenir of this momentous time.

Miriam wanted more. "We're a real group now! We should do a video!"

So we set up the camcorder in the classroom, and during lunch hour, all of us rehearsed a routine to the song "U Know What's Up." For the recording, the girls dressed in panda ears and T-shirts, and I danced in panda mode—well, for most of it, anyway.

We played it back after school and couldn't stop laughing. It was so fun to watch. The video was fuzzy and blurry, and we were out of sync most of the time, but it was still awesome. My friends and I were unstoppable—and making loads of money.

We were the 4*Townies!

"Ride or die!" we cried.

The 4*Townies were sitting on the bleachers during lunch hour, making key chains. We had run out of panda merch that morning, and we needed more. A lot more.

Priya whined and wanted to take a break. A *break?* What did she think—4*Town tickets would fall from the sky? "No pain, no gain, Priya! C'mon! Chop-chop!"

I was busy counting the money we had made that morning. "Five, ten, fifteen . . ." *It'll be all my fault if we don't have enough.*

Miriam tried to comfort me. "Girl, relax."

"Yeah, we're doing our best," said Abby.

"But it's not enough!" I cried. I got so mad that my panda paws, ears, and tail poofed out. My friends got quiet and looked my way.

I finally finished the totals. "The concert's this Saturday, and we're still a hundred short! *Augh!* I *knew* we should have charged more for the photos!"

We might not make it to the concert. Plus I have put so much time into hustling I haven't studied. For the first time ever, I got a C on a test. All of that for nothing! "Stupid, stupid . . ." I muttered.

Miriam scooted over. "Mei! Breathe. It's in the bag!"

I was still upset. "But—"

She put her arm around me. "What's the point of going to the concert if you're too exhausted to enjoy it?" I had to admit she was right. "Now take a break and help me appreciate some boys," she suggested.

I laughed. "Okay, okay, okay."

Miriam, Abby, Priya, and I watched a group of boys playing basketball nearby. The guys caught us looking, and my friends and I tried doing pickup lines and whistles. We were kinda lame at that stuff, but it was fun.

"You guys are so weird!" someone with a familiar obnoxious voice shouted below us.

Tyler was lurking beneath the bleachers. He called out that he wanted to talk to me. I told him to buzz off.

"Fine," he said. "Wonder if your mom knows her

precious little Mei-Mei's been flaunting the panda all over school."

That twerp! I raced down, ready to strangle him. I heard a huge *poof* and there were pink clouds surrounding me.

Tyler saw me coming at him in full panda mode and fell to the ground, frightened. Then he whipped out his cell phone and held it out: it had a photo of me as a panda. He had evidence. "O-one more step and I'm telling her everything!" Tyler stammered. "Now put that thing away and hear me out."

I begrudgingly calmed down and poofed back into a girl. I still didn't trust him, though.

He told me he wanted to throw a birthday party for himself—"an epic one." He showed me the invitation. "It's this Friday. If you're there, everyone will come. Simple as that."

I wasn't sure.

He sighed. "Look, I've done you a favor by keeping my mouth shut. All I'm asking for is one back."

It was an intriguing offer. It had possibilities. I could attach one important condition. "I'll do it," I said. "But it'll cost you one—no, two hundred bucks."

"Okay," he said, unfazed.

I hadn't expected that. I scrambled back to the bleachers to talk it over with the gang. With this money, we could go to the concert! My friends weren't crazy about the idea, though, particularly Miriam.

"Are you serious? You can't trust him," she said.

Abby called it a trap.

Priya had other issues. "This sounds like a boy-girl party. Are we allowed to go to boy-girl parties?"

"Guys, two hundred bucks will put us over the top! We *have* to do this. We'll meet at Tyler's, I'll do my thang, and then we'll bounce! Easy-peasy!"

Miriam still wasn't sure. "Dude, what about your mom?"

"I'll be back before she even knows I'm gone." I had gotten this far without her suspecting a thing. This was gonna be a piece of cake.

Before Miriam had a chance to argue, I called Tyler over. "We're in," I said to him. "But you get the panda for an hour, and we're not bringing any presents."

Tyler agreed to it, and we shook hands. The deal was sealed.

I was floating on air the rest of the week. Nothing could bring me down! With Tyler's cash, the 4*Townies would have more than enough money to see 4*Town. It was only a matter of time until I'd be seeing Robaire—in person!

On Friday I went home and put away my stuff. The plan was for Miriam, Abby, and Priya to get to Tyler's party first. They would set the stage for the panda. Then I'd make my appearance. Just one hour of panda-monium, and we'd be set.

My parents were in the kitchen, cooking.

"Okay, I'm heading off to Mathletes! See ya later!" I called out.

Mom shouted back, "Wait! What about dinner? I made all your favorites."

I looked toward the kitchen. The table was covered with awesome dishes, like Chinese pancakes, eel fried rice, and tangyuan soup. Mom and Dad had gone all out.

OMG . . . My stomach growled, but I had to go. I made up an excuse that Miriam's dad was ordering pizza. (Yeah, right. As if pepperoni and cheese could compare to Dad's delectable fried scallion pancakes.)

Then the weirdest thing happened: Mom said she wanted to tag along. "What are you doing? Linear equations? Geometry?"

I told her we'd be okay without her, but she followed me out of the house. I couldn't get rid of her. She listed her qualifications like she was applying for a job. "I was Mathletes champ in grade eight, you know."

I groaned quietly. *Can you puh-lease drop this?*

I told her that *Jade Palace Diaries* was on (I didn't even know if it was true), but that didn't stop her. *Was Mom always like this?*

We were headed to the front gates of the temple. I was sweating bullets. I couldn't have her following me. "Mom, you really don't have to come!" I pleaded.

"Don't be silly," she said. "We're already on the way—"

"But I don't want you to!" I blurted out.

We looked at each other, stunned. I couldn't believe I had just said that. Neither could she.

All of a sudden, we heard loud chatter behind the temple gates. Women were cackling and speaking Cantonese. Their voices grew louder.

"What's going on?" I wondered. Mom seemed confused, too.

The front gates burst open. In the doorway stood Mom's side of the family: Auntie Ping, Auntie Chen, and Mom's cousins, Auntie Helen and Auntie Lily. They formed a middle-aged fortress in front of us. Light from their collective bling scorched our eyes. Mom looked stunned, like a deer caught in the headlights of a gleaming sports car.

They all started talking.

"Look! It's Mei-Mei!" cried Auntie Chen, barreling toward me.

Auntie Ping greeted me, too.

Auntie Helen called out to my mom. "Hey, Cuz! We're here! Surprise!"

"Ming! Yoo-hoo!" said Auntie Lily.

The women swarmed me like bees. They took turns pinching and poking me, like I was a melon at the market. It was all overwhelming.

"Aunties!" I finally said. "What are you doing here?"

"The ritual, silly!" replied Auntie Ping.

Then Mom tensed up. She was looking straight at the gates. The aunties quieted down, and a stately figure swept into the courtyard.

"Mother!" Mom blurted out.

The aunties fell back, hushed. They separated and cleared a wide path for her as she made her entrance.

"Hey, Grandma," I said meekly.

The elegant woman strode toward me and took my face in her hands. "Poor dear," she said, inspecting every inch of it. "It must be so difficult keeping that unruly beast at bay."

Grandma finally took off her sunglasses. Up close, I saw a scar on her face. "Your family is here now, Mei-Mei," she said. "And we will take care of everything."

I heard Mom gulp.

My grandma and aunties marched to the house and took over our living room. They spread themselves out, setting down food, bags filled with gifts, and items for the ritual. The women smelled like pricey hotels and expensive perfume from the duty-free shop.

Mom tried to keep calm, but I knew she was seconds away from completely losing it. "What a surprise. You all came so early," she said with a weak smile.

"You need all the help you can get," Grandma said. There was a coldness to her voice. My grandmother sat proudly in the lounge chair as she spoke. She had the vibe of a queen on her throne. Dad was serving refreshments and handed her a cup of tea.

Meanwhile, Auntie Ping took a piece of fruit from Dad's tray and shoved it into my mouth.

"Eat," Auntie Chen ordered. "You need your strength

for the ritual." She noticed my hair and stroked it. "Your hair's so thick, like a pelt."

My relatives had brought all kinds of gifts for me, like candy and packs of cards. Mom told them they didn't have to, but it seemed like any time she said no, they brought out more stuff. I couldn't stand being there. I really didn't want all the attention. I felt like the main attraction at a petting zoo.

"Have you been managing to keep the panda in?" Grandma asked, eyeing me.

I said I had, but Auntie Chen's daughter, Lily, frowned. "Hmmm. Really?" She sounded suspicious.

Mom immediately stuck up for me (*You go, Mom!*) and asked what she meant by that.

"It's a little hard to believe that Mei-Mei could control such a beast. She's just a child," her cousin said.

Auntie Lily liked to brag about her own family. Whenever she visited, she made comments about how unruly other people's children were, not like her own perfect daughter, Vivian. *Uh, right.*

"If Mei-Mei's panda is anything like Ming's . . ." Auntie Ping said.

All the aunties shuddered. What was wrong with Mom's panda?

Mom stood right by me. "Mei-Mei's better than any of us at controlling the panda." Then she told them I passed every trigger test, including the kitten box.

Stunned, my relatives gasped.

Even Grandma was impressed. "The kitten box? It's so irresistible."

Mom beamed at me and tucked back a strand of my hair. "She just thinks of my love for her, and it gives her the strength to stay calm."

Ooh, boy . . . she still doesn't know the truth. Now she's bragging about me.

I looked up at Mom and gave her a small smile. "Exactly."

I glanced at the time. It was so late! I had to get to Tyler's party. I turned to everyone and yawned a few times, pretending to be tired.

"Anyway, thanks for all the gifts, but I think I'll go to

bed early," I told them. "Keepin' that animal locked down sure takes a lot of energy!"

"Okay, sweetie. Get some rest," Mom said.

Once I was in my room, I raced around, getting ready. I shoved all my stuffed toys under the blanket and shaped them into a big pile, like a body double, in case Mom checked up on me.

Then I started climbing out the window. I was halfway through when I heard a knock at the door. *Ack!* I scrambled back in again.

Grandma swept into the room, as composed as ever. "Mei-Mei, can I have a word with you?" she said slowly. She took out a handkerchief and unfolded it. Inside was a tuft of red fur. "I found this."

My throat got dry. She'd found me out.

"Strange for a girl who hasn't let her panda out." Her voice sent chills down my spine.

I acted like it wasn't mine, but Grandma didn't buy it. She studied the piece of fur in her hands. "I know how hard it is to keep the beast in. It feels so good to let it out."

I held my breath as she threw the fur into the garbage can.

She turned to me, darkly, and gave me a warning: every time the panda came out, that side of me got stronger. If I kept letting it out, I might never get rid of it. She said the ritual could fail.

I swallowed hard. "Has that ever happened?"

"It cannot happen," she answered.

Then she looked away. "Your mother and I were close once, but the red panda took that away." She touched the scar on her face.

Whoa! That's how she got it. Mom never told me.

"I couldn't bear to see that happen to you. So no more panda," Grandma ordered. She paused and contemplated a photo of Mom and me. She gave one last warning. "You are your mother's whole world, Mei-Mei. I know you'll do what's right."

Then she turned and left the room.

What am I going to do now? I paced back and forth, trying to find a way out. The clock was ticking: I was already late for Tyler's party. If I didn't go, we wouldn't have the money for the tickets.

But I couldn't panda out again. Like Grandma had said, it would be tougher to get rid of it. And she didn't know how many times I'd already gone full-out panda. I couldn't risk doing it. Besides, I couldn't let Mom down.

I looked at Wilfred for inspiration. *What do I do?*

Then—*ka-zing!*—an idea hit me. I scrambled out of my bedroom window. There was a way I could go to Tyler's party *and* get the money *and* keep everybody happy. And I didn't have to poof into a panda to do it.

I hurried off the bus and ran to Tyler's house. As I went up the front path, I noticed that the lights were on, but I

173

didn't hear any noise. The house was still. I looked through the window. Kids from school were hanging around the living room, looking bored. Priya stood in the middle of the room, imitating a snake molting its skin. Tyler had thrown the world's deadest party. Well, that was all going to change.

I rang the doorbell.

"Ugh, it's about time," Tyler said as he opened the door.

I was panting and gasping for air. I had raced to the temple and gotten out my old panda costume from the back room. On the ride over, I had slipped it on and done up the straps.

I went inside. "Yo! What up, peeps?" I shouted to the entire party.

People's faces fell. Tyler took one look at me and cried, "What are you wearing?" He was furious, threatening to call off our deal. "I'm paying for the red panda, not this garbage!"

I panicked. "Wait! Can garbage do this?" I showed off some moves from 4*Town videos. They didn't like it.

Kids were shouting, "Where's the panda? We want the panda!"

I had to get them to like me. I did other moves. "C'mon, guys, stir the porridge!" I shouted as I held my arms out in front of me and circled my hips. No one was interested. *Geez, this dance killed when I did it for the grade three talent show.*

My friends yanked me away from everyone.

Miriam seemed worried. "Are you feeling okay?"

I wasn't. I was freaking out. None of it was working. I didn't want to disappoint my friends, but there was too much at stake. "I just can't panda anymore. I'm sorry!"

I crumpled to the floor. This was a nightmare.

"You don't have to do it," Miriam said, rushing to comfort me. She told me they'd figure out a solution.

"I won't go," stated Priya.

"What? Priya!" I exclaimed. "You can't not go! Jesse's your soul mate!"

"But we only have enough for three tickets," she argued.

Abby volunteered to stay back next. I wouldn't let her. It was my fault that we didn't have enough money. I told them I would stay home.

Miriam stopped us. "Guys, if we can't all go, then none of us should go, right?" The 4*Townies sighed. We leaned against each other, on the verge of tears.

No! We won't give up our dream because of me, I thought.

"Just one last time," I said quietly to myself.

I turned around. "Hey, Tyler! You want the panda? You're getting the panda!"

Immediately there was a *phwoom* and pink clouds. The panda had returned.

"Let's hear it for the birthday boy!" I shouted, and hoisted Tyler onto my shoulders. Kids started cheering. The music was cranked up, and soon the party kicked into high gear.

The 4*Townies did everything to make sure people had a good time. I saw Tyler dancing alone in a corner.

I ran over and dragged him to the middle of the living room. "Come on, you're the birthday boy!" Miriam,

Abby, and Priya joined us, and other kids started dancing along, too.

Soon Tyler was the star of the party. "This is awesome!" he shouted.

I gave Tyler and the other kids rides on my back. "Faster! Faster!" Tyler shouted as I raced around his backyard.

Everything was working out the way we wanted. Tyler got the party he had hoped for, and Miriam, Abby, Priya, and I were going to see 4*Town. Nothing was going to stop us!

My friends and I took the leftovers of Tyler's birthday cake and went up to the roof to celebrate. There was a beautiful half-moon that night, and we could see lights twinkling all over the city. Abby brought along a radio. Miriam, Priya, Abby, and I kicked back, gulped down pieces of cake, and looked at the moon. Right then, there was nowhere else I would rather have been than on that roof, with my friends.

"Hey! Anyone seen Mei?" We looked over the edge. Tyler was in his backyard, searching for me.

"Dang! He is *working* you!" noted Priya.

I'd given rides to half the kids at the party. Apparently, that wasn't enough for him. I was too happy to care. It was all going to be worth it. The next day we were going to see 4*Town. I put my hands behind my head and settled back to soak it all in. And—*poof!*—I was back to being a girl.

Tomorrow's more than just a concert, I thought. *It's our first step into womanhood. It was our dream to go, and we made it come true.*

I remembered that I had put Robaire Junior in my pocket before I had left the house. I took the little game from my pocket and whispered, "It's happening, Robaire Junior! You're finally gonna meet your daddy!"

"And your hot uncles!" cried Abby. Then we all broke out laughing.

Miriam was next to me, thinking something over. "Mei," she began, "what if you didn't go through with the ritual? What if you kept the panda?"

What did she mean? I had to go through with it.

"Look at you!" Miriam exclaimed. "You're not the same feather-dustin', straight-A goody goody." She thought I was a new me—the real me.

Priya added that they had never gotten to see me before the panda. "Like ever."

Abby was behind them, too.

"You're such a rebel now!" said Miriam.

I guess it was a lot of fun breaking the rules and taking charge. It was awesome doing things together with the 4*Townies. But this was only temporary, until the ritual took place.

"Guys, I can't be like this forever. My whole family would freak, especially my mom." I sighed. "All her hopes and dreams are pinned on me."

Miriam smiled at me. "I know, but you've really changed, and . . . I'm proud of you. Just don't get rid of all of it, y'know?"

"If it weren't for you, Mei, none of this would be happening," added Abby.

It made me tear up. My friends were so proud of me. But I was proud of *them*! We moved in for a group hug.

"Friends. For. Life!" we shouted to the moon, to the stars, to all of Toronto.

As we hugged, the radio DJ came on. Once again, he mentioned the upcoming 4*Town concert in Toronto on the twenty-fifth.

We all froze. *What?*

"They'll be crankin' open the stadium dome and performin' under a red lunar eclipse!"

I immediately turned to Abby. "You said the concert was on the eighteenth."

She whipped out the concert flyer from her pocket, and we crowded around her. "Uh, this says Toledo," said Priya.

She was right: Toledo on May eighteenth, Toronto on May twenty-fifth.

"What the heck is Toledo?" Abby exclaimed.

No, no, no. This can't be right.

"4*Town's the same night as the ritual. . . ." Miriam said, her voice trailing off.

Phwoom! I poofed immediately. "Nooo! The same night? *The same night?*"

My friends tried to calm me down.

"It's okay," Priya said.

"No, it isn't!"

I felt dizzy and clutched my head. This was a disaster.

I couldn't miss the concert. But I couldn't let my family down, either.

"Hey! Panda Girl!" yelled someone with an incredibly obnoxious voice below.

I fumed. *What does that little twerp want from me now?*

Tyler saw me looking over the edge of the roof. "What're you doing? We want more rides!" he demanded.

I was tired of dealing with him. "Buzz off, jerkface. I'm *busy*!"

Kids started snickering. "You gonna take that, Tyler?" one said.

The laughing only made him angrier. "You want your money? Then get your butt down here *now*!"

Who does he think he is? I leaned over the edge and snarled.

Miriam tried to pull me back. "Mei! Let's just go!"

My entire body tensed up, and I was ready to pounce.

Tyler mentioned our deal, and I told him to forget it. "Shove your deal!"

"Fine, get outta here!" he yelled. "Go back to your psycho mom and your creepy temple, you *freak—*"

With a giant roar, I leaped off the roof, straight at Tyler. I landed on top of him.

"Take it back!" I screamed. "Don't talk about my family like that!"

I throttled him with both paws.

He screamed for help. "I'm sorry! Don't hurt me! I'm sorry!"

"Mei-Mei, stop! *What is going on here?*"

I looked up and saw Mom, out of breath, standing over me and holding her car keys. Horrified, she stared at me.

I suddenly realized what I was doing. I looked back at Tyler. He was shaking.

"I'm sorry," he whined. "Get offa me, please."

His head was bleeding. I had scratched him.

Meanwhile, the party had gone silent. I looked up. All the kids were gaping at me.

Tyler's parents were furious when they got home. They saw Mom at my side and blamed her.

"I cannot believe you would let your daughter do this," cried Tyler's mother.

"Do you understand what she did to my boy, huh?" said his dad.

Mom apologized over and over again. She tried to calm them down. "I'm so sorry. She's never done anything like this before."

Tyler's dad told everyone the party was over and they had to go home. Mom came toward me, and I braced myself for a big lecture. Instead, she passed by and went up to Miriam, Abby, and Priya.

"I can't believe you girls would use her like this!" she exclaimed.

My friends stared at me in shock. They tried to say it wasn't their fault, but Mom wouldn't listen.

"I knew you were trouble, putting all these thoughts into Mei-Mei's head, parading her around! Now she's lying, sneaking out—she attacked a defenseless boy! You think this is a joke? Do you know how dangerous this is?"

Miriam spoke up. "W-we didn't mean to . . . w-we just wanted to see 4*Town. . . ."

Mom was even more outraged at the mention of 4*Town. When Miriam said I had done it on my own, she went ballistic. "Don't blame her! Mei-Mei is a good girl, and you've taken advantage of her!"

Miriam pleaded with me. "Mei! Tell her."

Everyone was staring at me—my mom, my friends. What would I say to Mom . . . that I'd been lying to her all this time? That she couldn't trust me anymore? Instead, I said nothing. I turned away from my friends.

"Come on, Mei-Mei. Let's go," Mom said.

She held out her hand to me, and I took it. I couldn't bear to look at Miriam, Abby, and Priya as we left.

In the car, Mom told me that she had gone into my room and found the fake body double along with Tyler's invitation and the panda merchandise under my bed.

"From now on, you are to stay away from those girls." She squeezed my hand one last time before driving off. "You're safe now, Mei-Mei. Mommy's taking care of you."

Miriam, Abby, and Priya went crazy with joy: Robaire wanted to sign the 4*Townies to his label and be their manager. The group said yes right away. This was a once-in-a-lifetime opportunity.

While everyone was celebrating, Mei left the auditorium. She had been keeping a big secret. Robaire saw Mei and followed her. He asked if something was wrong. Mei told him she couldn't be part of the 4*Townies anymore. A big record company had already approached her, and she had signed a contract with them. She was going to be a solo artist.

Robaire was shocked. "I can't sign the band, then. I need all four girls. I have to find another group. The deal is off."

The 4*Townies were furious when they found out. "How could you do this to us?" cried Miriam. "We're your best friends." Tears filled her eyes. Priya was so angry she refused to talk to Mei, and Abby had to be placed in a straitjacket because she threatened to punch a hole in the wall.

"I have responsibilities," Mei pleaded with the girls. "You don't understand."

"Go back and turn them down. Tell them you're one of us!" Miriam said.

Mei looked at her friends. "I can't do that."

"Don't talk to us ever again!" shouted Abby in her straitjacket.

"You're not who we thought you were, Mei," said Priya at last.

They all turned and walked away, leaving Mei alone.

I stopped writing and closed the notebook. My heart was breaking. I looked around my room for Robaire Junior. Then I remembered that the last time I'd seen him was on Tyler's roof. I checked my pocket, and he wasn't there. *I must've left him behind.* I sighed. *Great, now everything's awful.*

I felt bad about so many things—lying about the party, poofing out again, scaring Tyler. But none of that compared to letting my friends take the blame.

Once we had gotten home, I had gone straight to my bedroom. Mom offered to make me some tea, but I said I was fine.

She kissed me on the forehead. "I found you just in time, Mei-Mei."

When I was alone, I took the notebook from my backpack to write one last fanfic. When I read it over, I realized it needed one more sentence:

"Guys, I'm so sorry!" Mei cried.

I had to stay at home until the ritual was over. Mom picked up my assignments from school, and unless I was accompanied by a family member, I couldn't leave the temple grounds.

"It's best this way, Mei-Mei. You'll be safe, surrounded by family," Mom explained over breakfast. "Your grandmother had recommended it earlier. After what happened last night, I have to agree. You should be with family now. Those girls were dangerous. You have to be careful about who you choose as friends, Mei-Mei."

I stayed in my room with Wilfred for the morning and moped. Then Mom knocked on my door and told me Grandma and my aunties wanted to take me out for dim sum. I wasn't exactly thrilled.

"Please don't pout, Mei-Mei," Mom said. "They're your family, and they are here to support you. After all, they came all this way because of you."

My aunties chose a new restaurant in Scarborough rather than downtown Chinatown. It was huge and had dozens of tables. I didn't see the usual dim sum carts with women calling out the dishes. ("That is so old-school," Grandma sniffed.) Instead, a sleekly dressed server took our order and brought the food to our table.

As Auntie Ping poured the tea, Grandma asked, "Mei-Mei, how is your Chinese coming along? Are you going to Chinese school?"

I swallowed a mouthful of cheung fun. "I started last year," I said, "but then things at the temple got—"

Auntie Lily interrupted. "How do you say 'hello' in Cantonese?"

"Lay ho ma!" I said proudly. That was easy. I knew a lot of Cantonese.

Auntie Helen looked at me. "Now how do you say it in Mandarin?" she asked coolly.

I took a guess. "Um . . . ni hey?" We never spoke Mandarin at home.

Auntie Helen smiled weakly. "Ni hao," she said, correcting me. She turned to the rest of the aunties. "She doesn't understand a thing!" she whispered across the table. "It's all Greek to her."

Auntie Chen put down her teacup. "What has Ming been teaching this child?" she asked my grandmother, beside her. "She is letting her run wild." She lowered her voice. "Do you remember the trouble Ming's panda caused?"

Grandma rolled her eyes. "Of course I do." Her fingers fluttered to her temple. "Don't remind me."

"*Ai-ya!* The temper on that one!" Auntie Chen exclaimed. "And you couldn't have predicted it. Ming was such an obedient girl."

"I still have nightmares," said Grandma.

All four women at the table shook their heads and shuddered. I could hear the gold fillings in their mouths rattle. I still couldn't believe Mom's panda had been that bad. My mother would never hurt anyone. But the scar on Grandma's face was proof.

Auntie Chen nodded. "It just shows you never know what lies underneath," she said smugly, and poured herself some tea.

Mom had told me once that Auntie Chen was jealous of Grandma. When they were growing up, Auntie Chen had secretly hoped she would end up in charge of the temple. Instead, the temple went to Grandma and her side. No one could argue with how well Grandma ran it. When the whole family got together now, Auntie Chen liked to drop comments about how successful her children were, but everyone knew Mom was the one the Chinese community in Toronto looked up to.

"I didn't mind my panda, actually," said Auntie Ping, smiling. "When the ritual took place, I was sad to see it go."

Everyone stopped and stared at her. "Are you saying you wanted to keep your panda?" Grandma sneered. It was the kind of voice that could freeze water.

Auntie Ping laughed nervously. "I meant I didn't know what I was doing!" she sputtered. "I was young! Foolish! Of course I didn't want to keep it!" She grabbed an egg tart and stuffed it into her mouth.

"I couldn't get rid of mine fast enough!" cried Auntie Lily, who was munching on a giant steamed pork bun. "The day of the ritual was the best day of my life."

Meanwhile, the server arrived with more food. She placed on the table some warm bamboo baskets of deep-fried dumplings, more steamed buns, and a large plate of vegetables gleaming with dark brown oyster sauce. It smelled good. We all reached in with our chopsticks. Auntie Helen took out her handbag and pulled out a tissue to wipe her brow. When she thought no one was looking, she dropped a pork bun into her open purse.

Grandma didn't say a word about her own panda. Like Mom, Grandma was very poised, but she was super strict. I always thought Mom was a bit afraid of her. My grand-mother sat straight in her chair, with perfect posture. I watched her fiddle with the thick jade bracelet around her wrist. Mom told me that the bracelet was Grandma's talisman. It was hard to believe there was a panda spirit trapped in there.

"I am just thankful the family made sure I went ahead with it," said Auntie Helen before taking a sip of tea. "I was very afraid."

My heart skipped a beat. "Is the ritual scary?"

Auntie Chen turned to Auntie Helen. "Don't scare her!" she whispered.

"You'll be fine," Auntie Ping said to me. She pointed to her stomach. "Be sure to breathe from the belly."

"Compared to giving birth, the ritual was a breeze," added Auntie Lily.

Grandma sipped her tea carefully and brushed away a crumb from her jacket. Finally, she spoke. "When this is over, we have to start planning Mei's future. Clearly Ming cannot handle this alone." Her mouth was firm. "First off, we should get her a tutor."

The aunties nodded in agreement.

Auntie Chen turned to me and smiled sweetly. "Mei-Mei, how about we get you a tutor? You'll like it! You can practice your Chinese. What do you think? You want a tutor?"

It was like she was offering me sprinkles for my sundae.

"I have two tutors for Vivian, one for Chinese and one for Japanese," Auntie Lily said. "It will help with her applications for college. They are looking for international experience. And she's going to start a third language soon!"

"Good idea!"

"It's never too early!"

I thought about my protest work with the 4*Townies. "Actually, I might not have time. I've got school and temple. And lately I've been really busy doing environmental action."

Grandma gasped. "Pardon me?"

Time for some environmental education! "My friends—Miriam, Abby, and Priya—and I are deeply involved in educating young people about the overwhelming crises in the environment. It's all because of society's lack of concern for the natural world."

It felt amazing to talk about causes that were important to me. It was finally Mei time!

"We are overfishing our oceans and seas. Dolphins and whales are headed towards extinction because of the industry's practice of net fishing. Not only that, we are polluting our waters with mankind's unlimited use of plastics. My friends and I created a petition to ban the use of plastic bags at our local grocery store. We got over two hundred signatures!"

The aunties were speechless.

"This is how you spend your time—talking about sea animals and plastic," said Grandma slowly. Her eyes narrowed. "That's all very good, Mei-Mei, but you should focus on your studies. You are still a child."

"This is our future!" I declared. "The fate of our planet rests on the actions we take today!"

Everyone stared at me, horrified.

"*Ai-ya!*" exclaimed one auntie under her breath.

Auntie Chen leaned over to my grandmother and whispered, "This ritual can't come fast enough."

Grandma closed her eyes and nodded.

The morning of the ritual, I couldn't stay still. I paced my room until I wore the carpet down. The ceremony was going to take place in the courtyard that evening. I kept checking the clock with dread. It felt like I was getting ready for the guillotine.

Mom came to my room. "Mr. Gao is in the court-yard," she told me. She suggested I join him for a chess game. "It might take your mind off things."

I got dressed and went to the temple. Mr. Gao was at his usual spot at the chess table. He waved me over. "Mei, we are long overdue for a rematch!"

I had known Mr. Gao since I was little. He owned the herbal store in Chinatown with his wife. He was a respected figure in the community. He was a nice man, if a little spacey at times.

We lined up our chess pieces. Mr. Gao made his opening move and waited for me. "I hope you're all set for the red moon ritual," he said cheerfully. "That panda of yours is pretty fierce."

My mouth dropped open. "Wait, you know about it? But how?"

"Know about it? I'm the one conducting the ceremony," he said, chuckling. He saw the look on my face and laughed again. "I've done a lot more than sell herbs these past fifty years," he said. "I guess your parents didn't tell you."

"That's nothing new," I grumbled. "They don't tell me much."

Mr. Gao took off his cap and wiped his brow. "They were trying to protect you, Mei, let you lead a normal life as long as possible. There are many dangers to the panda."

Like losing all your friends. I moped.

I made a dumb move in the game, and Mr. Gao took my king.

"Not up to your usual standard," he said, holding the piece in his hand. "This is a difficult time for you, but in a few hours, it will all be over. I promise."

I didn't say anything.

"Remember, Mei," he continued, "there are more good things to life than bad. You just may not recognize them as good at first."

I wasn't sure what he was talking about. But he was right. At least this would be over soon, and I could go on with my life—whatever that would look like.

Before the ritual, my family held a big dinner in the temple courtyard. My aunties scoured the best restaurants in Chinatown and brought back a feast: steamed whole pickerel with ginger and garlic, abalone and sautéed spinach, sliced barbecued duck, heaps of giant crab legs, and more.

My family sat around the table with Mr. Gao, talking and eating. But I took a look at all the dishes and sighed. I barely touched my food.

Suddenly, a giant 4 lit up in the sky near the stadium. I knew what it meant, and my heart sank.

Mir, Priya, and Abby must be at the concert right now, I thought gloomily. *They'll probably never speak to me again.*

Grandma saw the light and gasped. "What is that?"

Mom looked uncomfortable. "Um . . . I think it's coming from the stadium, Mother."

Grandma shook her head. "Four is the worst number."

Four was considered unlucky by a lot of Chinese people, because it sounded like the Chinese word for *death*.

My mother threw me a dark look. She knew what this 4 really meant.

Mr. Gao took a seat beside me. He was wearing special robes for the ceremony. "Nervous, Mei-Mei?"

"A little," I said. *More like a lot.*

He reassured me by reminding me that he had fifty years' experience as a shaman. "This will be a piece of cake," he said, chuckling. "And mostly painless." He reached for some barbecued duck.

"Thanks, Mr. Gao." *Hold on—did he say "mostly"?*

Grandma stood up and clinked her glass with chopsticks to get our attention. Everyone immediately stopped talking.

She began her speech. "Long ago, the spirits blessed the women in our family with a great challenge. Mei-Mei, tonight is your turn."

I tried to stay calm as my heart raced.

"Like all the women around this table, you, too, will banish the beast within and finally become your true self." She ended her speech, asking Sun Yee to keep me safe.

The aunties murmured their approval. Mom gave me an encouraging smile.

Mr. Gao looked at the sky and announced that it was time for the ritual. "The red moon is about to begin."

People began clearing the dishes, and Mom told me to get ready. I had to change. I walked past Dad, and he smiled at me. I smiled back but not for long. I wanted to be brave about this, but I couldn't hide my real feelings from him. I never could.

I went to my room to put on the ritual outfit over my regular clothes. There was a simple robe first, then an elaborate outer one. The robes flowed down and hid every part of my body—and who I was.

I smoothed them out and checked myself in the mirror. *This is the last time I see the whole Meilin, panda and everything.* My mind went back to the party and to scaring Tyler out of his wits. I flinched. I still couldn't believe I had done that.

The panda had to go. I had no choice. I took a breath and readied myself. It was time to grow up. Seeing 4*Town wasn't the first step to womanhood. This was.

There was a soft knock on the door, and Dad came in.

"I'm almost ready," I told him.

He looked at me, then looked down. In his hand was his camcorder. "I found this on the table downstairs." He chuckled. "I was wondering where it had gone."

Dad showed me the screen. "Did you make this?" he asked gently.

It was a goofy video the 4*Townies had made while we were hustling the panda. Miriam, Priya, Abby, and I were hugging and dancing and being silly. My panda form took up most of the frame.

I told him I'd erase it, but as I reached for the camcorder, he pulled it away. *Why did he do that?*

"We were just being stupid," I said. He didn't answer.

I planted myself by my bed. Dad sat down next to me. I had to get rid of that panda. I had attacked someone. What did it matter that I'd made some dumb video with my friends?

Dad looked at a photo of me and Mom. "What has your mom told you about her panda?"

"Nothing. She won't talk about it," I said.

"It was quite destructive . . . and big. She took out almost half the temple."

Whoa! No one had told me that. "You saw it?" I asked.

"Only once," he said quietly. "She and your grandma had a terrible fight."

When I asked what the fight was about, Dad chuckled and pointed to himself. "Your grandma didn't approve of me. But you should have seen your mom. She was . . . incredible."

Mom fought with Grandma about Dad? Hey, that's pretty cool, I thought.

Then I came to my senses. What did it matter? I had hurt someone. I had been crazy with anger. I had to get rid of that part of me.

"I'm a monster," I said.

Dad looked at me kindly. "People have all kinds of sides to them, Mei. And some sides are"—he paused and searched for the right word—"messy. The point isn't to push the bad stuff away. It's to make room for it, live with it."

He handed me the camcorder. He took a last look at the video. "Erase it if you want. But this side of you made me laugh."

I held the camera in my hands. My friends and I were on-screen, goofing around, having a good time. Dad appreciated this part of me.

I turned to him. "How come Grandma didn't like you? You're the best."

Dad chuckled again. "Your mother comes from a very influential family. Family ties are important to your grandma." He scanned the photos of Mom on the wall. "I emigrated from China when I was a teenager. Your mom

and I met in high school. She was quite a catch back then."
He glanced at me and smiled.

Eww, gross.

"I wasn't like the boys your grandmother wanted for her," he continued. "I didn't want to be a doctor or an engineer. Your mom and I had a long talk about it one day. We took the subway to High Park and talked until night-fall. She asked me what I wanted to do with my life, and I told her, 'I just want to make you happy.' "

That sounded just like Dad. I took a last look at my panda in the video. Pretty soon I was going to give all that up.

"Mei-Mei?" Mom called out. I quickly hid the camcorder. She opened the door, looking anxious. "It's time."

The temple courtyard had completely changed. The tables and chairs were gone, and lanterns and candles lit up the darkness. I smelled the thick scent of burning incense. My family and Mr. Gao were waiting for me. The aunties held old Chinese instruments in their hands. Their faces glowed in the silent courtyard.

Mr. Gao stepped forward. "Just follow my directions and breathe."

He led me to the center of the courtyard and told me to kneel. With a piece of chalk, he drew a large circle around me. I wasn't allowed to move from it.

He explained that the circle would open to another realm. "As long as the red moon shines, the Astral Realm will be open. And this circle is the door."

Mr. Gao motioned to Auntie Chen, and she struck a metal bowl. The pinging sounds reverberated in the air. My other relatives joined in on their own instruments and began chanting in Cantonese. It seemed strange and mysterious.

"What are they saying?" I asked Mr. Gao.

"The door will open only if they sing from their hearts. It doesn't matter what," he replied.

He told me to focus on their voices. My nerves were jangling under my skin. I closed my eyes and tried to steady myself.

Mr. Gao called out to Sun Yee. "Guide this girl through her inner storm."

Suddenly, the wind picked up and gusted through the entire courtyard. My skin grew warm, and heat surged in my chest. My body was light as air, and I could feel my legs gently leaving the ground. My body tilted back in midair: I was floating.

Mr. Gao told everyone to sing louder. He held a coin sword out to the blood-red moon, and a bolt of light blasted from it to my forehead.

"Return the red panda spirit from where it came!" he cried.

I shut my eyes tight. I felt swirls of energy wrap around me. It felt like I was falling through a deep tunnel.

When I opened my eyes, I found myself standing in a lush bamboo forest. The air was clear and damp, and the bamboo stalks soared hundreds of feet high. Mr. Gao and my family had disappeared. I was alone.

A gust of wind pushed me forward, and I made my way past the leaves and branches into a clearing. A bright light, gradually changing its form, lowered from the sky.

"Sun Yee," I gasped quietly. She looked as serene as ever. I bowed to her, and she did the same back.

Sun Yee waved her arms broadly, making a ribbon in the air. She formed the ribbon into a circular mirror. I looked into it and saw my own reflection. But the Mei looking back at me had regular black hair. The red was gone.

I tried to touch the mirror, but my hand went through it like water. When I reached in, a red panda paw passed through at the same time from the other side.

This mirror shows how I am divided, I realized.

I yanked my hand back. I looked to Sun Yee for

guidance, but she didn't show any emotion. I was going to have to go through this myself.

I took a deep breath and pushed through the mirror with both hands. *If this is what it takes to get rid of my panda, I'll do it.* As I stepped through, it felt like electric shocks were raining on my entire body.

"Aaaahh!" I cried.

I pushed through the mirror with everything I had, but it was a struggle. It felt like my limbs and body were being strangled. I heard a loud roar. I looked back and saw my panda spirit unleashed, resisting with fury.

All my memories of the panda flooded back: hiding from Mom in the bathtub, being hugged by the 4*Townies in my bedroom, racing home in a panic from school, leaping onto Tyler in a rage, dancing with my friends on video.

I had so many feelings with the panda: happy, sad, angry, excited. They were all part of me. Every piece belonged to the jigsaw puzzle. For once I saw who I really was.

Then it hit me: *I don't want to give this up. I want to keep all of it.*

Suddenly, I stopped pushing. I didn't want to go ahead with this. I wanted to stay the person I was, the good and the bad. After all, this was the real me.

I had made my decision. I climbed back through the mirror, leaving the Astral Realm behind.

I landed with a thud on the ground. Huge plumes of dark pink clouds surrounded me. I squinted and looked around. I was back in the temple courtyard. And I was the panda—*Yes!*

Everyone was coughing from the clouds.

As the air cleared, Grandma stared at me, astonished. "Mei-Mei?"

One by one, my family realized I still had the panda.

Mom immediately said, "It's okay. We can do it again." She reached out to me.

I shook my head and backed away from her. "I'm keeping it."

Grandma shrieked. *"What did she say?"*

The aunties couldn't believe it, either. "This girl has gone soft in the head!" one of them declared.

"I'm keeping it!" I repeated. Then I turned away and started running.

My family and Mr. Gao came after me. They tried to grab me.

"What's come over you?" Mom cried, struggling to hold on to me.

"Get a hold of her!" Grandma ordered.

The aunties tried to tackle me, and for a moment, all I saw were designer labels clutching my fur.

"No, Mei-Mei! STOP!" Mom demanded.

"Mei-Mei, listen to your mother!" Grandma yelled.

"No!" I roared.

I managed to shake them off, and they all stumbled to the ground. I heard something crack and splinter. Mom's talisman was missing from her neck.

"I'm going to the concert!" I announced. Then I headed to the temple gates and fled.

"Get back here!" Mom cried.

But I didn't look back. She was talking to Mei-Mei, and Mei-Mei didn't exist anymore.

34

I raced to the stadium. I could still make it there in time. More importantly, I had to make it up to some very important people. The 4*Townies were special to me, and I had to let them know it.

Managing the streets of Toronto was a piece of cake. I had learned to harness the poof power. To get more speed, I poofed in the air as a girl, with the pink clouds propelling me through the air. Then I made a soft landing on the ground in my panda form. Easy peasy!

The stadium came into view, and fortunately the roof was open. I turned off the main road and gathered steam. Finally, I took a huge running leap toward the stadium and soared into the air like a superhero.

I landed on top of the stadium dome and peered inside. Every seat in the stadium was filled. Fans were holding huge 4 signs and screaming for the Magical Four Plus One. Luckily, one girl screamed louder than everyone else. I could recognize Abby's roar anywhere, and I zeroed in.

I leaped into the stadium and managed a perfect landing. Right before I reached the ground, I poofed back into a girl. Pink clouds swirled around.

"Mei?" asked Miriam and Priya, coughing.

"Mei!" Abby cried. "You're here!"

Miriam immediately wanted to know why I was there. She seemed wary. I couldn't blame her.

I tried to catch my breath. "I couldn't do it. The panda's a part of me. And you guys are, too."

Miriam looked hesitant. "Mei, you threw us under the bus," she said, upset. She turned her back to me.

"I know, and I'm sorry. I've been obsessed with my mom's approval my whole life. I couldn't take losing it." Tears came to my eyes. "But losing you guys feels even worse."

Miriam wouldn't even look at me. "Well, too bad, because you did."

I sighed. *Maybe it's too late.*

Then I heard familiar beeping sounds. "Robaire Junior?"

Miriam reluctantly pulled my game out of her pocket.

"Here," she said. "Found him at Tyler's."

I had thought I'd never see him again. I was so happy to have him back.

"She's been taking care of him twenty-four seven," Priya said, teasing her.

"And singing lullabies to him every night," Abby added.

Embarrassed, Miriam turned red. "No, I haven't," she sputtered. "They're lying."

I moved to hug her. Miriam hesitated at first, then smiled and hugged me back.

"4*Town forevah?" I asked.

"4*Town forevah," she said.

Abby and Priya joined us. Soon we were in a big group hug, which is the best kind ever.

As we were hugging, I heard Miriam say, "Tyler?"

We all turned around. There was Tyler Nguyen-Baker

on the concert floor, decked out from head to toe in 4*Town merch.

Tyler turned bright red and pretended not to know us. He faked a deep voice. "Tyler? Who's Tyler? I don't know a—"

"You . . . are . . . a . . . 4*Townie?" I couldn't believe my eyes.

Tyler froze. *OMG, he's just as big a fan as we are.* Then we squealed and ran to hug him. He squirmed and tried to get away, but we wouldn't let him.

"He's one of us!" I cried. I rushed to apologize. "I'm so sorry about what happened at the party. Do you forgive me?"

Tyler shrugged and nodded. "Yeah, whatever." Meanwhile, he was getting the full 4*Townie treatment. Abby had him in a playful headlock while Miriam and Priya were tousling his curls. "Hey, don't mess up my hair," he called out, laughing.

I could tell he was going to fit right in.

Miriam pulled me aside. I could barely hear her above all the noise. "Your mom must've gone nuclear!"

"Who cares!" I answered. "What's she gonna do? Ground me?"

The whole group cracked up.

All of a sudden, the stadium lights dimmed. That could mean only one thing: the concert was about to begin.

Chants of "4*Town! 4*Town! 4*Town!" echoed throughout the stadium. The 4*Townies screamed so hard my eardrums almost popped.

A glowing 4*Town sign topped the stage, the giant 4 shining like the North Star. It had been my lifelong dream to see them, and now it was happening. I could hardly breathe.

The jumbotron lit up, and a countdown appeared. Miriam, Priya, Abby, and I huddled close together.

The crowd shouted out the numbers on the screen. "Four . . . three . . . two . . . one!"

The lights onstage beamed, and five cages rose from

beneath the stage. Each cage held a different member of the band. The jumbotron flashed stadium-sized pictures of 4*Town on-screen. My heart beat like crazy. Here they were, live, in person. This was better than I'd ever imagined.

"Yes!" the 4*Townies cried together.

The singers rattled their cage bars, struggling to break out. They were trapped. Then, one by one, the cages burst open. Each 4*Town singer finally stepped out, free: first Aaron T and Aaron Z, then Tae Young, then Jesse. There was only one cage left.

"I'm gonna barf!" yelled Abby. "This is the best day of my life!"

The last cage flew open, and Robaire finally appeared. "Toronto!" he called out. "Who knows what's up?"

The crowd roared. As 4*Town left their cages, a pair of wings unfurled from the shoulders of each of the singers.

"OMG, they're angels!" Miriam cried. "That's so perfect!"

Then the music started and Robaire began singing the first notes of "U Know What's Up."

Fans surged in waves toward the stage.

"C'mon, let's go!" I shouted to my friends.

We joined the crowd and pushed across the concert floor, moving closer with every inch to heaven on earth. As their wings spread, 4*Town rose into the air. People screamed even louder.

Priya grabbed hold of my shoulder. "Please don't let me pass out. I don't wanna miss this."

Robaire looked into the audience and held out his hand. It seemed like he was singing only to me. As we got closer to the stage, I reached out my own hand. The 4*Townies saw me and lifted me up, getting me closer to Robaire. It was like a dream. I was near the stage, and my fingertips were stretched way out. Robaire held out his hand toward mine. Our fingers were about to touch. . . .

"Mei-Mei!"

I looked up at the sky and saw the face of a gigantic red panda at the edge of the stadium roof. There was a swoop to her hair that I immediately recognized.

"Mom?"

Mom searched for me. "Mei-Mei, where are you?" she roared.

The crowd screamed at the sight of her. Robaire, Jesse, Tae Young, Aaron T, and Aaron Z dangled from their wires, clearly terrified.

Mom scanned the crowd and spotted me in the audience. She shouted for me again, and I started running. *What's she doing?* My friends were right behind me.

Dust and debris showered down. Everyone was fleeing for the exits. Mom climbed into the stadium.

I looked at an exit and saw my family fighting to get in.

"Mei-Mei!" Grandma shouted.

"Out of the way, people! Family emergency!" yelled Auntie Helen, elbowing the mob.

Mom made a gigantic leap from the rim of the roof and crash-landed close to the stage. Debris lashed the concert floor. She stood upright, and I saw her full size. She must've been almost three hundred feet tall. *Mom's ginormous!*

I heard my name and turned around. My dad was running toward me.

"Dad?" I cried.

My entire family, along with Mr. Gao, caught up to me. They were wheezing. They looked horrified. Then they started speaking all at once.

"We have to save your mother!" Grandma exclaimed.

"We have to do the ritual again!" Dad said.

Suddenly, an enormous shadow loomed over us. I looked up and saw a huge paw coming down straight for me.

"Mei-Mei!" Mom roared, grabbing me. Her paw wrapped around me and pulled me into the air.

"Noooo!" I screamed.

My family shouted at Mom to let me go.

"Ming! She's your daughter!" Auntie Lily exclaimed.

Mom wouldn't listen. "You are in big trouble, young lady!"

I squirmed and struggled, but she wouldn't let me out of her grip. My friends yelled at her to stop.

Tyler joined in, too. "Let her go! You Momzilla! You psycho bath mat!"

But there was no stopping her.

Mom clomped to the stage. "I'm shutting this down right now!" She reached for the 4*Town sign and swiped it with her paw. The giant 4 crumpled like cardboard. Helpless, I watched as it crashed to the ground. I'd lost my North Star.

"Mom! No!"

Then Mom turned, roaring, to the crowd. "Everyone go home! Where are your parents? Put some clothes on!"

She reached again and tore down the rest of the sign. My heart broke. She had damaged the scaffolding holding up the set, too. Suddenly, 4*Town was swinging over the crowd like out-of-control puppets.

Then in one final swipe, Mom took out the 4*Town jumbotron. The giant pictures of my idols vanished.

"Noooooo!"

This isn't real. This isn't happening. I looked around me. The set was totally destroyed. Everyone was crying out, panicking. The 4*Town guys were screaming for their lives. Even Robaire looked helpless.

All because my mother hadn't wanted me to go to a concert.

Mom looked down at me in her paw. *"This isn't you!"*

I curled my hands into fists. It was time.

"This . . . is me!" I cried.

Then I exploded into the panda and chomped down on Mom's paw with all my might.

Mom yelped in shock. I broke free from her paw and fell hundreds of feet. I landed on all fours with a *whump*. My friends and family rushed toward me.

Dad checked on me first. "Are you okay?"

The aunties quickly followed. "Mei-Mei, are you hurt?"

I was shaken, but I managed to get to my feet. I steadied myself and got ready for battle. I wasn't Mom's precious Mei-Mei anymore. Mei-Mei had left the building.

I looked up at Mom and yelled loud enough for her to hear with her oversized panda ears. "I *lied*, Mom!"

Stunned, Mom looked down at me.

"It was *my* idea to hustle the panda, *my* idea to go to Tyler's party. It was all me!" I'd been wanting to say that for so long. "I like boys! I like loud music! I like gyrating! I'm *thirteen*! Deal with it!"

My family and friends stared at me in disbelief. I'd finally shown who I was. Grandma ordered my family to stop staring and get the ritual ready. I had to distract Mom.

"Keep her busy!" she yelled.

"Oh, I'll keep her busy," I said. There was a lot more where that had come from. I was just getting started.

Mom tried to grab me with her panda fist, but I dodged her. Meanwhile, Dad was making a giant circle on the concert floor with a line marker. Mr. Gao was climbing the stairs to the top of the stadium.

"Lying to me? Biting me? How could you be so . . . so crass?" Mom roared.

"You wanna see crass?" I turned around and started popping my booty right at her. "You gave birth to this, Mom!"

Mom roared again. "What are you doing? Who taught you that? Put that away!" She staggered in pain, like the sight of my shaking booty burned her eyes.

My friends cheered me on.

"Destroy her with your big butt!" shouted Abby.

Dad finished drawing the circle for the ritual. "Start chanting! Now!" he shouted at my family.

Grandma and the aunties stepped up to the circle and sang, just like they had in the courtyard. But this time the circle barely flickered. That meant the ritual wasn't working.

Grandma ordered my relatives to sing louder.

"We're trying!" replied Auntie Chen.

I tried to stall Mom until the ritual began. I danced more. "Take it, Mom! Take it!"

Mom covered her eyes with her paw. "Stop it! Sto-oop!" Her gigantic tail thrashed everywhere, smashing into the decks of the stadium. The aunties ducked for cover. I tried to dodge it, but her tail smacked right into me. I held on for dear life.

"Aaahhh!" I screamed.

My whole life she's been telling me what to do. No more! I started climbing furiously. I shinnied up her tail and climbed onto her back, poofing in between. "All I wanted . . . was to go . . . to a concert!"

Mom tried grabbing me but missed. "I never went to concerts. I put my family first. I tried to be a good daughter!"

I poofed and landed on Mom's face. I dug into her fur with my claws. "Well, sorry I'm not perfect!"

I poofed again, hovering above her head as a girl.

"Sorry I'm not good enough! And sorry—"

Poof! I panda-ed out and hurtled towards Mom.

"I'll never be like you!" I catapulted forward, and with a giant roar, I butted Mom right between the eyes.

Mom stumbled and staggered, then crashed to the

ground. I fell and tumbled over. All my limbs hurt, but I managed to get back on my feet.

Mom was out cold. She lay flat on her back outside the ritual circle. The circle's light was waning. Then it went dead.

"Mom! *Mom!*" I cried.

I looked at the sky. The red moon was almost gone.

I ran toward Mom. "Mom! You have to get into the circle!"

I grabbed her tail with both paws and tried to pull her gigantic frame. "Wake up," I pleaded. "I'm sorry!" She wouldn't budge. Even with all my panda strength, she was too heavy for me.

"Please!" I wailed.

I caught sight of Grandma taking off her bracelet. She closed her eyes and smashed the bracelet on the ground.

Meanwhile, I was still trying to get Mom back into the circle. It was the only way we could do the ritual. But it was no use. I wasn't strong enough.

"Pull, Mei-Mei!" someone next to me said.

"Grandma?"

Grandma had poofed into a red panda. *OMG, she's a panda, just like me.*

Grandma stared at me with determined eyes. "I'm not losing my daughter." She yelled to the aunties, "Don't just stand there!"

One by one, the aunties came running, smashing their talismans as they raced toward us. Suddenly, four red pandas who kinda resembled my aunties surrounded me.

Auntie Chen took charge. "Make room for your elders, Mei-Mei!" she said, jostling me aside to take hold of Mom.

"We're with you!" Auntie Ping exclaimed.

I was speechless. "What're you doing? What if you can't turn back?"

Mom's cousins shrugged it off. "She's family!" cried Auntie Lily.

"Your mom needs us!" Auntie Helen added, grunting as she dragged Mom.

We all pulled together, slowly inching Mom into the circle.

Grandma cried out, "Start chanting!"

The aunties obeyed, but the circle flickered only a bit, then sputtered.

"Louder!" Mr. Gao exclaimed. "Sing from the heart!"

Dad looked our way. "Louder!" he repeated. "The circle isn't working."

My heart ached. *Mom might never change back because of me.*

Right then, I heard beatboxing—bad beatboxing—from the concert floor. It was Miriam. Abby and Priya were doing it, too. And Tyler was drumming along to the beat. My friends were helping out.

Then, from high up, someone started singing "Nobody Like You." I recognized that angelic voice. *No way, it can't be . . .*

I searched the stadium. Perched on top of a mountain of debris was Robaire, singing the greatest song ever recorded. The other 4*Town members joined him. This was unbelievable. I wanted to cry. My friends, my family, and my favorite band in the world were trying to save my mom.

Suddenly, the circle burst into a fierce glow. Fans who'd been hiding under their seats came out and joined in the singing. My relatives and I kept pulling, slowly heaving Mom into the circle.

Dad pointed to the sky. "He made it!"

Mr. Gao had scaled to the stadium rim. There was only a small sliver of red moon left. He lifted the coin sword to the heavens.

A bright red shaft of light beamed down, striking Mom in the center of her forehead. The circle glowed brighter and brighter. The ritual was working! Fierce winds blew around us, shaking the walls of the stadium.

I felt myself being lifted. Mom, Grandma, and the aunties were floating, too. Then came a blinding flash . . . and the whole world went dark.

When I opened my eyes, I was back in the bamboo forest. Soft green light filtered through the bamboo stalks. I breathed in the crisp air and calmed down. I hadn't realized before how peaceful it was to be there.

But I was all alone. "Mom? Mom!" I called out. She was supposed to be there with me.

I made my way through the bamboo, pushing away leaves and stalks. Someone was crying in the distance. *Is that . . .*

I started running toward the sound. *"Mom!"*

I saw her on the ground, her shoulders hunched. Her hair was long, red, and sloppy over her shoulders. She looked defeated.

I went up to her quietly. "Mom, are you okay? We have to—"

She looked up, and I gasped. It wasn't Mom's face—not the one I knew. This girl looked only a few years older than me. She wore glasses. She seemed startled to see me there.

"Mom?" I said.

"I'm sorry," she said. "It's all my fault. . . ." She started sobbing.

I kneeled next to her. I tried to be reassuring. "What is? What happened?"

"I–I hurt her . . ." she said, and wiped away tears. She seemed as timid as a rabbit.

I asked her who she had hurt.

"My mom," she answered. "I got so angry . . . and I lost control." She started crying again.

Grandma's scar. This is how it happened.

"I'm just so sick of being perfect," she blurted out, frustrated. "I'm never going to be good enough for her. Or anyone."

Why didn't she tell me before? Maybe things could've been different.

I comforted her and smoothed her hair. I was used to

seeing Mom perfectly groomed. There was never a hair out of place.

"I know it feels that way, like, all the time," I said as a tear slid down my cheek. "But it isn't true."

We gave each other a small smile. *I think you're good enough, Mom. We're family.*

I got to my feet and held out my hand to her. "C'mon," I said gently.

Mom took my hand, and I guided her through the trees. It felt like the walks we had taken when I was little, when we wandered the streets of Chinatown. I would hold on to her with my tiny hand. But this time I had to be the grown-up.

As we walked together through the bamboo forest, she slowly changed like seasons, from teenager to young woman, then finally the woman I recognized as my mother.

I heard the aunties squawking ahead.

"We have to find them!" cried my grandmother.

They ran toward us when Mom and I reached the

clearing. My relatives were in human form but with red hair. They all started talking at once.

"You're okay!" wailed Auntie Ping.

"Finally! We have to hurry!" said Auntie Chen.

Auntie Helen and Auntie Lily told us we had to get out of there.

"Ladies."

My relatives got quiet, and Grandma swept in between them, as regal as ever. She came up to me and Mom. Ashamed, my mother looked at the ground. I could tell she was bracing herself to be yelled at.

My grandmother looked at Mom. Then, without warning, she gave her a hug. Mom was surprised—in a good way.

"I'm sorry," Mom said, hugging Grandma back.

"You don't have to apologize," my grandmother said. "I'm your mother."

Then Grandma turned toward me. I held my breath. She gave me a nod. "May Sun Yee guide you and keep you safe."

Things were going to be all right after all.

The mirror was in front of us. One by one, my family went through. As each one stepped into the mirror, her panda spirit pulled away and disappeared into the forest.

Finally, it was Mom's turn.

I squeezed her hand. "Go ahead. It's okay."

Mom stepped through, and her panda spirit was released. But then she looked back through the mirror at me and broke down.

"No, Mei-Mei, please!" she shrieked. She held out her hand. "Just come with me!"

I didn't take her hand. I wasn't going to join her. "I'm changing, Mom. I'm finally figuring out who I am, but"—I teared up—"I'm scared it'll take me away from you."

"Me too," Mom replied. "I see you, Mei-Mei. You try to make everyone happy, but you are so hard on yourself. And if I taught you that, I'm sorry."

This wasn't the same Mom as before. This wasn't the same me.

"So don't hold back," she continued, "for anyone."

She placed her hand against the mirror. I did the same on the other side, our hands touching.

"The farther you go . . . the prouder I'll be," said Mom.

I wanted to say the same thing to her.

As the eclipse ended, the mirror, along with Mom, faded from view. I was alone in the forest.

I turned around, and Sun Yee appeared in front of me. "I'm not going to regret this, am I?" I asked.

Sun Yee smiled the happiest of smiles. Then, in a swirl of mist, she poofed into a gorgeous red panda. She swooped straight at me.

Poof! I joined her as a panda, and she carried me up. Together, we floated free in the sky, gazing at the beautiful full moon.

The fans were on their feet for a standing ovation. The 4*Townies bowed and bowed as the audience cheered. This was the final night of their world tour. Each city had sold out. The 4*Townies gave endless interviews and made TV appearances nonstop.

The tour almost hadn't happened. But Mei had told the record company she was a 4*Townie forever, and the company had let her out of the contract. Miriam, Abby, and Priya had welcomed Mei back with open arms. They signed with Robaire right away.

After the show, the girls immediately started talking about their next projects.

"Let's do a movie!" cried Abby. "We should do a martial arts movie with lots of fighting!"

Priya suggested doing a supernatural fantasy movie, of course.

"How about a TV show?" Miriam said. "We can do a reality series about the 4*Townies."

Mei took charge—again. "Remember, guys, it's not just the four of us anymore. There are five of us now. Whatever we plan from now on, we have to include everyone."

A new member had recently joined the 4*Townies. Just like the original 4*Town, their band now had five members. They were one big happy group: Miriam, Abby, Priya, Mei, and their mascot, Tyler.

"What?" Tyler cried out, reading the story. "Why am I the mascot?"

"It's a joke!" Laughing, I took back the notebook. "I'll rewrite it." I put the notebook in my backpack. "Besides, you're one of us now, Tyler."

Miriam closed her locker and came up to us. "Yup, you're a fully-fledged 4*Townie," she said, and rested her elbow on his shoulder.

Tyler smiled and shrugged. "Yeah, I guess it could be worse."

School had just finished, and the 4*Townies were hanging out in the hall.

I checked the time. "Oh, crud! I have to go. Catch you guys later, right?"

"See you!" Priya called as I rushed out of the school.

A while later, I hopped off the streetcar and ran to the temple gates. I said a quick hello to Bart and Lisa and waved to Mr. Gao in the courtyard. After all he had done for me at the ritual the previous month, I had been letting him win at chess.

Mom was kneeling at the altar when I rushed in. I took my place next to her and bowed my head.

Beep! Beep!

Mom looked down at Robaire Junior, which she wore as a pendant around her neck. "This thing is hungry all the time," she said with a sigh.

Because her pendant had broken, Mr. Gao had put Mom's panda spirit in the nearest thing he could find. Mom was lucky. Grandma's panda spirit had been placed in something a little less subtle. She blamed her bad luck in mah-jongg on the giant 4*Town necklace she now had to wear.

We had lots of tours booked that day, so Mom and I got going. I still worked at the temple, but after the ritual, I had gotten a different role.

Mom and I went to the gates, and I did a quick *poof*. Then we opened the doors. Crowds were lined up as far as we could see.

Mom introduced the Lee Family Temple. "Yes, we are home of the Great Red Panda. Here she is!"

I greeted everyone. "What up, Toronto!" I shouted. "Get in here!"

Things had never been better at the temple. Sometimes we couldn't keep up with all the traffic. Dad helped out with tours (and wore my old panda costume—I think he found his calling), and I was always ready for photo ops. We got loads of panda merch at the gift shop, and the donation box was usually overflowing. Good thing, because we somehow had to pay to rebuild the stadium.

The 4*Townies showed up at the front gates.

Miriam called out to me, "Ready to get your karaoke on?"

I was more than ready! I finished up and ran to them, poofing back partway. I liked to keep the panda ears and tail sometimes, 'cause it was rockin'.

Mom saw me and glared. "Hold on. You're not going out like that, are you?"

"My panda, my choice, Mom," I called back. "I'll be back before dinner, 'kay?"

Mom relaxed. "Fine," she said. Then she asked my friends if they wanted to come over for dinner.

"For Mr. Lee's cooking? You bet!" Miriam said.

Mom was even teaching my friends how to make dumplings. I wouldn't have been surprised if she'd tried to get them to watch *Jade Palace Diaries* next.

As we went past the temple, my friends stopped and checked out a photo that was hanging in a place of honor in the temple.

"OMG, you got it framed!" exclaimed Abby.

"It looks awesome!" Priya said.

Tyler agreed. "Yeah, it's pretty rad."

After the ritual at the stadium, we had taken the most epic photo in the history of mankind, with my family, my friends, Mr. Gao, and—OMG! I still can't believe it!—every member of 4*Town. They were the ones who had suggested it, too.

Robaire came up and told me that had never happened before at one of their concerts. (Yes, I got to meet Robaire!) He even told me my panda moves were pretty slick. I could've died on the spot! I stood right in the center of the photo as a panda, big as life. The whole band autographed it and signed it *To Panda Girl*.

Lately, I've been thinking. Ever since I turned thirteen, life's been . . . a lot. People still talk about Pandapocalypse 2002. Mom and I just call it . . . growing pains. Sometimes I miss how things were, but nothing stays the same forever. The number one thing I've learned is we've all got an inner beast. We've all got a messy, loud, weird part of ourselves hidden away. And a lot of us never let it out.

Sometimes people ask if I regret keeping the panda. I tell them no. All these sides make up who I really am. What good's a song if you can sing only half the notes? Sometimes people are happy with that answer, sometimes not.

Then I turn to the person with a question of my own:

"Isn't it time you let your panda out, too?"